A Season for Unnatural Causes

Stories by

Philip F. O'Connor

A Season for Unnatural Causes

ILLINOIS SHORT FICTION

Other titles in the series:

Crossings by Stephen Minot
Curving Road by John Stewart
Such Waltzing Was Not Easy by Gordon Weaver

A Season for Unnatural Causes

Stories by

Philip F. O'Connor

UNIVERSITY OF ILLINOIS PRESS

Urbana Chicago London

"The Pony Track" appeared first in *Discourse*, Autumn 1970, © 1970 by Concordia College; "Constants" in *Kansas Quarterly*, Winter 1971-72, © 1971 by *Kansas Quarterly*; and "The Thumb" in *Quartet*, Summer 1974, ©1974 by *Quartet*.

The author is grateful to Frederick Rinehart of the Mary Roberts Rinehart Foundation for a grant-in-aid in 1971 and to Bowling Green State University for faculty research grants during the summers of 1971 and 1974.

Library of Congress Cataloging in Publication Data

O'Connor, Philip F.
A season for unnatural causes.

(Illinois short fiction)
CONTENTS: The escape artist.—The disciple.—Fire.—The pony tract.—Cold places. [etc.]
I. Title.
PZ4.0194Se [PS3565.C64] 813'.5'4 75-2289
ISBN 0-252-00518-X
ISBN 0-252-00531-7 pbk.

For Delores
and for
Robert Early

Contents

The Escape Artist

She cupped her hands under her belly. In the morning she moved like a slug. By afternoon she was in bed.

"David. Bring me a carrot."

He hurried to the refrigerator, opened the vegetable drawer, shoved aside mushy things, found a carrot, ran it to her. "What else?"

"I don't know. I just don't know."

"Do you want to get up for a while?"

"In, phwfff, my condition?" Her arms were out, legs in a V, carrot stubs around her pillow, the belly a mountain.

"Jesus," he said. "It's big!"

"Do you think you have to tell me?"

Between bedroom and living room there was a mirror. Now, as often, he stopped to examine himself: grayish sad face, the bags under his eyes like supplicating hands, hanging shoulders, a shapeless paunch. *I haven't always looked like this*, he thought, moving on.

In the living room he went to the end of the sofa, turned around, backed up a few steps, bumped the arm and went over, landing heavily, face up.

From the hallway a sound: Buh blump! Buh blump! Buh blump! He turned toward the doorway.

In she came, a baboon on chicken legs. "Help me to my chair."

He twisted off the sofa, stepped over the books, slung his arms under her shoulders, steered her to her chair, started to set her down.

"Easy, please. Eeeee-seeee."

He lowered her by the inch. The chair exhaled. She nailed her heels to the floor and gripped the arms. Her eyes fell off to one side:

"A carrot."

He hurried to the kitchen, found one, big and fresh, ran it back.

"There's a funny old English movie," he said, fussing with the T.V. knob. "Peter Sellers. A labor boss. His wife complains all the time. He has a daughter with big . . ."

"I have no interest."

"It's nice to see you up anyway."

"No, it's not." She began to chew.

He turned away. He couldn't stand watching her. He couldn't stand listening:

Scruncchhh! Scruncchhh! Scruncchhh!

It didn't seem to be the carrot she was eating, but the back of his head.

Scruncchhh! Scruncchhh! Scruncchhh!

He watched the movie but couldn't concentrate. Finally he turned, said, "That's sure loud, Ellie."

Her mouth stopped at full circumference, went partly closed. "What's loud?"

"Your chewing."

She opened her hand. The carrot somersaulted down her belly and fell to the floor. "Help me up."

"What's the matter?"

"Up."

"Now, just a sec . . ."

"Up!"

He helped her up.

"Bed."

"Be reasonable."

"Move."

He propelled her from behind. He slid her through the doorway, across the room, released her at the bed. She twisted down among her droppings.

"Chewing," he said. "It's nothing. My remark meant nothing. I'll get you another one. A bunch. I'll sit here while you eat it. Everyone makes noises. Part of life. Just because I . . . said something . . . doesn't mean . . ."

One of her eyes was open, the other closed. The open eye reached up and punched him.

"Ellie?"

She hissed, said nothing.

On his way to the living room he stopped at the mirror, saw himself again: hair askew now, face grayer, eyes like the niche-eyes in an ancient statue. Only minutes had passed but he looked years older. He shook his head at the wonder of it.

Each afternoon he stayed late at his little office at the university, where he was a graduate assistant. He said he had extra papers to grade. There were no extra papers.

Kathy arrived. Long legs, large eyes, quick movements. She sat down in the chair beside his desk, looked across, said, "These ungodly people." She meant everyone but him: her dorm counselor, other students, the dean of women, teachers, the college president, her parents, even others. She stretched her legs out, looked at her sandaled feet, said, "I like coming here. I think you're like me. Spacey."

He didn't know what "spacey" meant but he nodded, not wanting her to know he didn't.

"Without these conferences I'd jump off something, I swear."

Ellie was a heavy fog over the region of McGrath, Kathy the rescuing sun. She had brought him poems again. She reached out to give him one. He accidentally touched her hand. He held it. The conversation stopped. She stared at him. He stared at her. He raised her hand and kissed the fingers. Then, abruptly, he put her hand on her lap and stood.

"Hey! That was nice! What are you jumping up for?"

He walked to the window, looked out at an elm. "I have responsibilities."

"Screw responsibilities."

"You don't understand," he said without turning.

"Maybe I don't," she said, "and maybe you're not as spacey as I thought."

Undergraduate talk. He would ask someone. *What, specifically, does spacey mean?* He turned back to her. "I'm as spacey as you are. But . . . but there are other considerations."

She winced.

"Temporary."

An uneasy smile.

"I'd say weeks, maybe a month, then . . . who knows."

"You have another chick and you don't want to fool around. That it?"

"Sort of." He didn't wear his wedding ring and hadn't told her he was married.

"What's she like?"

"Well, she's . . . fat."

"Yuk!"

"Terribly fat, but . . . but . . ." He turned back to the elm.

"You owe her something? That it?"

"Well, in a way."

"I understand."

How could she understand?

"Doesn't matter," she went on. "I'll keep dropping by. When I have poems. Okay?"

"Yes," he said, still not turning around. "Please."

She said she was going to leave a few more poems on the desk. He heard the clamps on her loose-leaf binder snap open. He heard them snap closed. He heard her walking toward him. He closed his eyes. She kissed the back of his ear. Then she left.

He'd get a Honda. And one of those broad-brimmed Ezra Pound hats that were becoming so popular. They'd go south, into Mexico. *What's your occupation?* the border officials would ask. *Poet*, she would say. *Explorer*, he would tell them. South they'd fly, his chin on the handlebars, her legs out like wings. They might go as far as Peru.

He watched her pass along the sidewalk under his window.

Space. Spacey. He, they, needed a lot of space. Was that it? His eyes followed the top of her head as if she might look up and answer. She disappeared behind a nearby building without looking up.

He returned to the desk, picked up the top poem of the several she had left on top of the desk:

All right, bastards,
Peel pennies from these broken hands
And fling them to the wind.
Strip me in the dust
And leave me for carrion.
Better such oblivion
Than the lives I've led for you.

He looked at the title, "Dark Legacy," and at the inscription beneath it: "For my parents." He didn't know whether he liked the poem or not, but it had qualities—gutsy, decisive—he admired. He put all of her poems in his briefcase and started for home.

Peru. Maybe even Brazil.

He opened the front door.

She was in her chair, legs out, her pale-green nightgown stretched to the limit.

"How's it been?" he said.

"I just threw up."

He had lately been searching for that mysterious word, gesture, or act that would somehow stop her pain. "Maybe I could massage your stomach or something."

"Don't touch me," she said. "I'm raw and sore."

She was holding the newspaper. The new resident in the apartment across the hall, a graduate student from India, had been picking it up, knocking on the door, and handing it to her. "Here is your newspaper, Meesus Mogroth. I do not weesh to see you bending over in your condition." His name was Mr. Moradaba. He was thin, had oily eyes, wore white dress shirts and loose-fitting suit pants. When he saw David coming or going, he bowed and said, "How do you do, Meester Mogroth. I hope today Meesus Mogroth is feeling herself much better." David had been giving him quick answers: "Fine."

"Yes, thanks." "Much."

"I see Mr. Moradaba brought the paper again."

"Of course. He's a gentleman, David." She was referring to the way David came in without picking up the paper. She'd remind him to go back outside for it. He'd forget. She'd have to pick it up herself.

"Well, at least I can read it to you," he said.

She held it possessively to her stomach, looked over the top, "It's one of the few things I can do for myself."

"I'll cook supper then."

"I can't eat. Cook for yourself. Or go out." She snapped the paper back and continued to read.

Sometimes he went to a hamburger stand near the campus. He'd go now except that he was very tired. Besides, something was worming around at the back of his brain, like one of those thoughts you had moments ago but now can't recall. It nagged him. It had something to do with Ellie. He'd chase it until it identified itself or went away. He took two books from the pile in front of the sofa and went into the kitchen. He opened one of the books and tried to read. He couldn't concentrate. He gazed into the blackness outside the window above the sink.

Maybe they should talk.

What would they talk about?

He imagined a conversation:

I've been seeing a student in my office. Frequently. A female. Today I touched her hand and didn't want to let go.

He sees her trembling in her chair. *Tell me you're lying, David. Tell me it's only a joke.*

I'm not lying, Ellie. I'm very horny about her and much in danger of falling in love. Is it possible that we, you and I, could work out some sort of arrangement, at least until after the child is born. After that . . .

She stands with great difficulty, right fist pressed against a place under left shoulder, moaning as if she's been shot.

Control yourself, Ellie. All needn't be lost. I may need only a short respite. We'll just have to work it out the best way we can. First of all . . .

She hobbles to the bathroom, falls across the bathtub, reaches for the leg-razor on the other side. He comes after her, falls on top of her. They grapple for the razor. He cuts himself but gets it safely away. He stands, then struggles to help her up, saying:

I'm sorry, Ellie, but the truth must come first. You've become, since the pregnancy, a terrible wraith. I can't stand being with or looking at you or hearing you or even smelling you and have just got to get away.

She is up, standing beside him, beating him on the head with the toilet-bowl brush. Shouting, *I'll kill you ten times over!*

He turned toward the living room. "What do you want, Ellie? Tell me and I'll get it for you."

"I want you to shut up and let me read the paper."

"That's all?"

"That's all."

He turned back to his book, which contained an assigned reading for the modern-novel course he was taking. He was supposed to be reading an essay on Hardy. There were several essays on Hardy. Which one was he supposed to be reading? He flipped the pages, back to front, found two of the Hardy essays: neither seemed familiar. He turned to the table of contents: six Hardy essays in all; nothing clicked. The essay had been assigned weeks ago. He'd remembered it as late as two days ago; now he'd forgotten. He flipped the pages front to back, thinking the opening paragraphs would give him a clue. He read all the opening paragraphs; no clue. He slammed the book closed, got up, went into the living room, stepped over his other books, sat down on the sofa. He looked across. When she turned a page of her newspaper, he spoke:

"Has the doctor figured out yet when it's due?"

"I've told you he can't give us a date."

"I thought maybe by now he'd be making guesses."

"He can't guess. I wasn't keeping track of my periods. He has no way of knowing." Her face had not appeared from behind the paper.

"It's got to come out soon," he said. "It can't get much bigger."

"Yes, it can," she said. "It can get much much bigger. It can go on growing for days, weeks, even a couple of months." She'd lowered the paper slightly. He could see her unfriendly eyes. "He doesn't know, David, and I don't know. My sickness has complicated it. In cases like mine it can be way overdue. And, whenever it happens, the birth won't be easy."

"I hope it's easy, Ellie."

"Do you, David? Do you really?" Her voice was full of disbelief.

"Yes, I do," he said sincerely. *And soon*, he thought, *oh very very soon.*

He picked up his notebook, which was on top of the book heap. He stared at it. He put it back, looked across. "What about your sickness?" he said, "Isn't *that* supposed to stop pretty soon?"

"It was supposed to stop weeks ago. And don't ask me what the doctor says because he doesn't know. It's not morning sickness. It's something else. And don't ask 'what something else' because neither I nor he knows that either. He's going to take tests but he thinks it may go on."

"That . . . that would be terrible," he said, sitting up.

Her eyes were now appearing and disappearing at the top of the paper. For the moment, he could see them both, aiming at him over the top of the paper. He couldn't see her mouth, which was now saying, "I believe you, David. Everything you say and do tells me how terrible you find my sickness!"

"I only said it because you would have to go through . . ."

"It *hasn't* stopped though, has it? That's the situation, isn't it? And it may not stop. It may go on after the baby is born. It may go on for a long time. It may go on for years. It may go on until I die. Who is to say it will ever stop?"

The highest building he could think of was the university administration building, seven stories. He saw himself going off the top in a two-and-a-half. He'd tumble down into a big black-and-white X painted across her immense belly. He'd splatter her and child across the quadrangle. But he would, miraculously, sadly, bounce and live.

"Do you have anything else to say?"

"No," he said. "Not just now."

He picked up his notebook. Again he tried to study. Again he couldn't.

The Indian. If he could get the Indian to do more than pick up the paper, he wouldn't have to rush home after classes each afternoon. He wouldn't have to hear or see her so much. Maybe he could pay the Indian to come in, clean up, and cook for her. *Easy on the curry powder*, he would say, *and heavy on the carrots.* He himself would stay in his office, meet Kathy, eat at the hamburger stand with her, walk her to the room she rented, have long talks with her. Ellie could let the Indian rub her back, or whatever she wanted. The Indian, the Indian's presence, would help her stop throwing up, would make life better for her. For him. Maybe, for the Indian.

"I guess you're right," he said.

"About what?"

"Mr. Moradaba. He's certainly a gentleman. He asks how you are every time I see him."

"He *cares* about others, David."

"People get that way living in an overcrowded country. You have to care or get trampled."

She didn't seem interested.

He'd try something else. He'd find a way to get the Indian to come in. Then he himself would disappear. How would he get the Indian to come in? He wasn't sure. He'd have to be subtle so that neither she nor Moradaba saw through the arrangement.

He closed his eyes.

He thought of Kathy, pictured her at a small desk, writing a poem.

Poems.

Moradaba seemed the sort who wrote poems.

He'd send poems in the name of Moradaba.

What poems?

He remembered composing lines here and there in his notebook. They might do to warm the way for the Indian. He turned a page, another, another. Finally he found a scribble, three lines, a verse, something. He peered down, read:

A cock in a sock,
A ball on a wall,
Ass in a glass.

Impossible! What had been going through his mind when he'd written that?

He turned pages, came across another:

How
I
Sizzle
When
You
Fart
&
Fizzle.

Och!

He turned more pages.

Lines here, lines there, all depressingly the same: scatalogical, obscene, pointless.

Kathy had told him she was merely a vessel through which the words flowed. If that was true of all writers of poetry, he was a sewerpipe. She had also said she relaxed and the words found their way out. He hoped he hadn't been relaxed when he'd written that filth in his notebook. No. He musn't have been relaxed. Real poetry would come when he relaxed. He'd wait, get himself into a lyric mood. Meanwhile he'd do something else. It would, after all, take more than poetry to get Ellie to invite Moradaba in.

What something else?

He sat quietly for several minutes, then turned to a blank page of his notebook. Within a half-hour he had written:

> Dear Mrs. McGrath:
>
> I can no longer refrain from speaking to you the truth. Your appearance in your doorway every day sends chills into my spine. I have been, without your knowledge, writing to you poetry. Is it not possible, at some discreet time, for me to spend a few precious minutes with you reading to you what I have written? I will serve to you a glass or two of only the sweetest wine and speak to you only in the mildest tones. Is there any harm in such? Oh, do make your

feelings known to me, secretly of course, at the most convenient time.

Sincerely,
A. Moradaba
Neighbor

Perfect.

And maybe he should try at least one poem for a starter. He turned to another page, thought, got something, printed:

Let us roll together
On a large pillow . . .

He wondered at the next word: *Under? Around? Over?*

He began again:

Let us roll together
On a large pillow
Gently over the moon.

Fine. He might expand it later, but if he couldn't, it was good enough. He'd walk around the block after leaving in the morning, then come in and slip both letter and poem under the door.

A beginning.

He looked up, said, "How are you feeling, Ellie?"

"How do you suppose I'm feeling?"

"Better, I hope."

"Like a sack of garbage. That's how I'm feeling."

He saw her to bed, returned to the living room, waited until he was sure she was asleep, went in, cleaned away the mess of carrots and crumbs on his side and got in beside her.

He felt relaxed. Words came:

. . . Gently over the moon
With a lot of other people . . .

. . . Gently over the moon
With a lot of other people
Who have nothing to do . . .

. . . Gently over the moon
With a lot of other people
Who have nothing to do
But screw and screw and screw.

It was positively a reject.

What kind of a husband am I, he thought, *encouraging, about to encourage, actually wanting, some sort of, not some sort of, the real thing, between my wife and another man, a man I don't know, a foreign man, a man who . . .*

He was asleep before he completed his question.

He hung his lower legs over the sofa arm. He clasped his hands behind his head. He closed his eyes. He thought these thoughts:

I am a heinous despicable man. Her tortures in this unwanted pregnancy have been doubled, if not tripled, because of me. I buy food I like and it makes her sick. I try to clean the apartment but it seems dirtier when I'm finished. When shopping I rush her in and out of the car and supermarket because I am ashamed of being seen with her. She wants her mother to visit but I have put her off because I can't stand that bitch and fear she will never go away. My words are spit on the face of my wife. My thoughts are jack-knives into her heart. The times I have cheated her in my brain are uncountable. I have imagined arrangements that would make of her a whore, a liar, a thief, a beggar. For these and for more I should be dragged through the streets, naked, tarred, an example for all other male tyrants, most of whom are probably saints compared to me.

As he thought these thoughts his penis rose against his fly and caused such pain that he loosened his belt, unsnapped his pants button and lowered his zipper. He looked down and watched his penis preen toward the ceiling. He turned away, tried to ignore it. Visions of girls had begun to step blithely between his sentences. Now they were stepping into them. He looked down in anger and disgust, watching himself grow. *There is no excuse for this*, he thought. *I am the most . . .* But the girls trampled his words. The sofa began to creak.

"David, what's that noise?" She was in the bedroom.

He didn't answer. He got up and, holding his pants with one hand, cradled himself with the other and hippety-hopped to the kitchen. He removed the cradling hand and scooped a handful of margarine. He hippety-hopped to the bathroom.

"David?"

He closed the door. He went to the toilet and bent over it. His eyes fell into the mirror, where he saw himself, hunched and hairy. He turned away and cupped his lubricated hand under his penis. He turned from the mirror and transformed the image of himself into another, a mocking picture of Ellie, bent with her belly, holding it up as he was holding up that which, for the time being at least, possessed him. *What an insult!* he thought. His pants fell. He brought his hand forward once, twice. *She doesn't deserve this.* Three times. Four. Splop! Splop! Splop splop! *I am an uncivilized dog,* he thought. *It's worse than murder!* Splop!

"David!"

"I'm flushing something down the toilet," he said. Lately he had been flushing everything down the toilet: food scraps, cigarette butts, napkins and the like. Now this!

His answer seemed to be enough. She didn't call out again.

He crept back to the sofa, fell sideways onto it and curled up. *I am less than worthless*, he thought. He felt his penis sink between his legs, pictured it: with a face, grinning.

He usually waited until Ellie was settled in for the night before trying to study. Sometimes, for a change of atmosphere, he went to his office or the library. Lately, unable to concentrate for long periods, he had been quitting early and stopping at a place called Margaret's Tavern.

He sat alone in a back booth, drank his draft beers slowly and spent a lot of time watching the girls who passed his booth. *This place suits me*, he thought more than once. He had four or five beers and was usually back in the apartment by ten.

One night a girl in a tight blue skirt sat against the edge of his table and, as she spoke to someone between booth and bar, shifted her weight from one cheek to the other. After watching the cheeks swelling and pulsating for several minutes, he saw his hand start slowly across the table toward them. It was like someone else's hand, a disembodied hand, a hand with a life of its own. As it neared the end of the table, it rose like the head of an ostrich and reared back, about to pounce. But just then the girl stood and walked away. Margaret, squat and fiftyish, was passing with a tray of empties and noticed the hand poised awkwardly in air. Her eyes moved to the girl, who was now walking toward the entrance with the young man she'd been talking to. Her eyes swung back to David. He pulled his hand back, looked into his glass, then apologetically up at Margaret. "One more draft, please," he said. Margaret hesitated, picked up his empty, and went to the bar. When she came back she put his beer down with a bang and said, "What kind of a place do you think this is?" He tried to give her a smile, couldn't, said he didn't know. "Well, *I* know," she said emphatically. "Just watch what you do in here." He nodded. She took his money and walked away.

He felt guilty about going to Margaret's without Ellie. A few times, when she was awake, he'd tried to get her to join him. He said the booths were big and comfortable and the yeast in the beer would do the kid good. She refused, saying the child was going to be a giant as it was and didn't need yeast. Besides, she said, she didn't like sitting in dumps. At such times he waited for excuses: she was having another long phone conversation with her mother, they needed something at the drug store or carry-out, he wanted to browse among paperbacks at the bookstore that stayed open late. He made his excuse, went to Margaret's, stayed an hour or so, came home.

He stopped getting home by ten after he first saw the Red Amazon.

One of Margaret's regular customers, she was an instructor in art, about six feet tall, with eyes like a wolf and hair that came flaming down over the shoulders of her silky dresses. The crowd seemed to part when she came in and glided toward her favorite stool at the end of the bar. She ordered a drink, usually something colorful and fancy with a straw sticking out of it, then turned sideways, crossed her bare legs and began looking about. When she spotted someone she liked, she kept her eyes on him until he came over and sat on the stool beside her.

David observed the action: her companions made helpless stupid faces, nodded or grinned whenever she spoke, and fumbled for money when she wanted another drink.

Once, just after she came in, she went to the ladies' room and, on her way back to her stool, slowed and looked at David. It was an intense look, but somehow a look without meaning. He wasn't certain. He gave her a little nod. She shrugged, went back to her stool and began, as usual, to survey the customers near the front.

On his way home that night, he thought about the Red Amazon. She was not the sort of woman he had ever seen. She was almost more than a woman. Maybe some new kind of woman. She was a kind of woman he wanted to meet.

Ellie was waiting with questions:

"Have a good time?"

"No."

"See anyone you know?"

"No."

"Anyone you'd *like* to know?"

"No."

"I don't believe you."

He went to the kitchen and made a cheese and baloney sandwich. He'd talk to the Red Amazon, then the edge would be off his fancies. He'd concentrate on his work. He'd start getting home earlier. He'd pay more attention to Ellie. He finished making the sandwich, got three carrots from the refrigerator, and came back to the living room.

"How's your stomach?" he said.

"I threw up in the bathroom sink. It was gray."

"Please."

"It smelled worse than ever. I think I'm going to do it again."

He put down his sandwich. In his stomach the beer gurgled. He made his way around the pile of books and sat down on the sofa, looked across.

Two wet eyes faced him: puddles, sinks, cesspools.

"I'm tired," he said, sensing something. "I think I'll go to bed." He started to get up.

"Stay," she said. "I want to talk."

He hesitated, then sank back to the sofa, knowing she would get him to listen, in the bedroom if not here.

"Do you remember when you told me I was pretty, David? 'God,

Ellie, you're a knockout,' you said. Remember?"

He remembered.

"Remember when we went water skiing up on that lake and afterwards, when we were lying on the sand, you said, 'You could be blind and deaf and mute, and I would still be totally happy in your presence.'?"

He remembered that too.

"Later I told you I'd been a quarter-finalist in *Miss Western Iowa*, and you said the contest was fixed or I would have won. Remember?"

He remembered it all.

"Would you say those things to me now, David? Would you?"

He might but he'd be lying.

"Look at me. Look at what I look like."

He did. A mess.

"Whose fault is this, David?"

"Mine," he said, knowing the answer she wanted.

"You're right," she said. "Yours as much as mine."

"Maybe more," he said, hoping she'd stop.

"Marriage is supposed to be sharing, the pains as well as the pleasures. What are you sharing with me, David?"

I have pains too, he thought.

"Do you think marriage is knocking a woman up and then, when she's pregnant, running off to a saloon to look at other women?"

He didn't. He shook his head.

"Well, that's what you *seem* to think it is. You go to your classes. You come home and help, but just a little, the minimum. Then you go off to that place and you can't stand *looking* at me. That's the worst part!"

"You're still a knockout, Ellie."

"Bullshit! But at least pretend."

"Well, I don't really have to . . . that is, I . . ."

She struggled out of the chair. She hobbled to the bedroom. She got into bed. Creakkkkooo, crack!

I'll pretend, he thought.

He rolled off the sofa, followed her to the bedroom, slipped out of his clothes and got in beside her. He reached across. His hand landed on her belly. Hard. Full of little bones. The bones were moving, violently moving, crabs fighting inside of a balloon. He moved his hand upward. Her breasts were full but felt ugly to the touch. He moved his hand higher. His fingers found her lips. They were tight, like the sides of a stretched rubber band.

"It's moving again," she said. "Leave me alone until it stops."

He withdrew his hand without hesitation.

"I can't stand it," she said. "You don't know what it's like."

He lay silent. He thought he should say something. He could think of nothing. The window was slightly open. He was looking through the window.

". . . just don't know."

Still and silent.

She stopped squirming about.

Soon she was asleep.

He imagined the Red Amazon coming naked through the window. She bellied across the floor, slipped in beside him. They kissed. She wasn't enough. He added two others, Kathy and one of the prettiest he had seen that night in Margaret's. He invented the contortion that made it possible for him to have all three of them, all of them each other. The Amazon's forest fell up against his mouth. *Bite me,* she said. He bit. *Harder!* she cried. He did it harder.

Ellie woke up. "It's quieted down now," she said.

The vision was lost. He rolled onto his back. He put his hand out. It landed on her forehead. He kept it there, flat, dead.

"What do you think you're doing, taking my temperature?"

He removed his hand.

"We can't do what you *want* to do," she said. "But it doesn't prevent you from touching me."

He rolled over awkwardly, catching her hair with his elbow ("Ack!"). He wrapped his upper arm around her stomach as far as it would reach. He felt the bony creature in her kicking at his arm. He closed his eyes and brought his face down to kiss her. He smelled vomity breath. He stopped up his nostrils, kissed her quickly on the cheek and drew back.

"Is that all?" she said.

He pulled out his hand and rolled onto his back.

"I don't deserve you, Ellie," he said, hoping he'd found something final, something that would stop the conversation before it started. "I just don't deserve you."

She lay quietly for a while. Finally she turned and said, "You're right, David. You *don't* deserve me."

A shaft of light slanted across his office, ending in a bright puddle on the floor near the wall. He was sitting low in his chair, facing pens, pencils, a few folders, a scattering of books and several sets of ungraded papers. He raised his eyes, followed the shaft of light to the puddle. It was creeping across the floor, would soon climb the wall. His eyes moved upward along the shaft, toward the window. The sunlight blinded him. He closed his eyes.

They live in a hut on a cliff above a beach. She wears only cut-off blue jeans and a white t-shirt, he only a pair of faded yellow shorts. Their bodies are brown. They write in the mornings. They swim in the afternoons. Lizards and harmless snakes also inhabit their hut. They are learning Spanish. Young people from the village come to visit them. At night they go to the posada. There they dance the native dances. She reads her poetry. Afterward they carry home with them quaint wine jugs the proprietor has given them.

There was a knock on his office door.

"I'm here," he said, sure it was she.

There'd been no appointment. She'd not come by for a week. But this afternoon she was coming by. He'd felt it all day. He'd tell her he'd felt it, the magic of it, speak of the silent communication that was possible between them. He'd say, *You are in pain,* because he had felt that too, her pain, her need to share it with him.

"The door is unlocked," he said.

The door opened slowly. A fat unshaven man in gray workshirt and pants stood scowling in the doorway. "When you leavin?"

"Oh." David lowered his feet from the desk. "What time is it?"

"Five-thirty. I wanna start in here. You gonna be in here for a while or what?"

"Give me . . . give me a half-hour."

The janitor sent his dull eyes about the room, as if looking for something that shouldn't be there. Then, apparently satisfied that he'd found it, or maybe that it wasn't to be found, closed the door.

They have written letters, invited others to join them. Now the others, couples and groups, live in similar huts along the beach. In the evenings they sing, talk and read poetry together. They raise animals and grow food the land will bear. Some of them write. Kathy is finishing a volume of poetry. He will go into the city and find an English language publishing house. He will use an imprint he and Kathy have invented: The Exile Press. *Hers will be the first book published.*

The phone's ring shattered a vision of himself with a backpack full of manuscripts, cycling over a dusty road toward the city.

He picked it up, hopeful. "Hello."

"Why aren't you home?" It was Ellie.

"Papers. I have some papers to grade and . . ."

"Stop by the drug store and get me some Amphogel tablets for my stomach and buy a couple of magazines, *Redbook* and something else." She spoke in monotone, seemed to be reading. "Write a note for my mother's birthday so I can put it in the envelope with my card. Say something nice so she thinks you mean it. We're going to have to go out and get something for her before she visits. Are you going to eat a hamburger or coming home?"

"Hamburger."

"I want those tablets soon. When will you be here?"

"Hour. Are you feeling all right?"

"I feel the way I always feel. You sound funny. Is someone there?"

"No one."

"I need those tablets. Don't delay. Goodby."

"Goodby."

Click.

He has smoked pot several times but it has made him dizzy and paranoiac and he is afraid of it but he will smoke it with Kathy and the others, do it the right way, not make the mistake of drinking wine at the same time which is why, he is sure, he got dizzy and para-

noiac. He won't take heavier stuff, mescaline and cocaine, even if the others do, because he is going to handle the business of the commune and will have to be alert and practical and . . .

The phone again.

He picked it up.

"I forgot to tell you to stop at the supermarket and get some carrots and coffee and bread and whatever else you think we need. And I also want you, when you write that note, to *invite* Mother to stay with us so she doesn't think it's just me and knows you . . ."

He had cupped his hand over his mouth. "Not person you think," he said in a low voice. He pictured the janitor, made him Russian. "He go in library. He say tell person who call he be home very late. Something he remember he have do."

"Can you leave him a note, in case he comes back?"

"No," he growled.

"Why not?" she demanded.

"Janitor not suppose to take messages. Goodby." He hung up.

Their most precious moments would not be with the others but with each other. Naked under moonlight, they would learn to touch in a thousand ways. They would talk into the dawns, take long trips to the mountains. They would find constant entry into each other, electric touches: more than common love, less than invasion.

The sunlight had passed from the room. He sat very still in his chair. He had, suddenly, an odd sense of her presence. He got slowly out of his chair, walked to the door, opened it, looked down the empty hallway. He thought of calling her, didn't, knowing now that she was nowhere near. He returned to his desk. *Afraid*, he thought. *I frightened her with my talk. She needs time to shed the fear.* He left the ungraded papers, picked up his briefcase, and started for the door. He stopped halfway, put down the briefcase, went back to his desk, opened a drawer, removed a sheet of paper and pencil, and wrote:

> Kathy-
> Door will be unlocked. Go in and call my home, no matter what time. Two rings. I'll know it's you. I'll get here.
> D.

He folded the paper in half, wrote a large K on the outside, took some Scotch tape from his dispenser, went over and taped the note to the door. He returned to his desk, got another sheet of paper, and printed:

JANITOR!
THIS IS IMPORTANT!
DO NOT LOCK DOOR!
DON'T FORGET!
D. McGRATH

He left the second note in the middle of his desk, picked up his brief-case and left, full of wishes, full of certainty.

The pile of books in front of the sofa had become a small hill which he could no longer crash through or step over but had to walk around. He'd added novels, books of criticism, and volumes of journals containing articles. *I ought to be reading these*, he thought whenever he passed them. Each time the instruction became more urgent.

There would be a midterm exam. When was it? Maybe Dr. Boggs had announced it in one of those classes he had missed when Ellie was at her sickest. But how many had he missed? He'd have to borrow notes from someone. He didn't know anyone in the class except to say hello. Still he had to get those notes. He'd have to say to someone, *Can you lend me the notes for the classes I've missed?* Then, if the other student said yes, he'd have to ask, *Do you happen to remember what classes I've missed?* How could he ask a thing like that? He'd have to compare the borrowed notes to his, then try to figure the missing parts for himself. That would be difficult. He hoped the borrowed notes were readable, not full of blank spaces and doodles the way his always were—arrows, guillotines, pocket knives and (more recently) pistols, rifles, cannons, tanks, and battleships. The rest were phrases and half-phrases, meaningless single words—the whole barely intelligible.

He was standing beside the pile, trying to remember the date of the midterm, when the phone rang. He went into the hallway and answered it.

"Where's Ellie?" The sharp voice of Mrs. Tanner, her mother.

He squeezed the receiver tightly in his hand. "Out," he said.

"By herself?"

"I had to go to class. She took a cab."

A pause, then: "It's just as well. There are some matters I've been wanting to discuss with you."

He tightened his squeeze, wishing the receiver would crumble to black powder in his hand.

"As you know, I didn't like the idea of you two getting married before you had your degree, and, while I was willing to go along with it because Ellie had confidence that you'd finish your course work and have a job by next fall, my doubts have remained, and, I don't mind telling you, increased, not only because of that untimely pregnancy of hers but also because I now understand you may not finish your course work by fall after all and may remain a student and live on that graduate assistant's salary throughout all or part of . . ."

He put the receiver down softly on the telephone book. He went into the bathroom and pissed. On the way back he looked through the kitchen window, toward the street—no cars. He returned to the phone and quietly picked it up.

". . . and though you may try to argue, as I am sure you have, to Ellie, that it's because of the child you won't be able to finish, I am going to argue right back to you the very opposite, by which I mean it's precisely *because* of the child and all the responsibilities of being a father that you *ought* to be completing your degree this year and not . . ."

He put the phone down again, shuffled to the living room and looked down at the books in front of the sofa.

He'd now remembered there was also a paper due. A paper on one of the writers. He'd had to put his subject on a note, which he'd handed to Boggs in the second week of the course. A writer and a book. But what writer? *Good God!* What book? Only he would know? But he didn't know. Only who knew? Only Boggs knew. He could call Boggs and ask him: *Who am I going to be doing my paper on?* But he heard Boggs's answer: *The one you are supposed to have been researching these past five weeks.* That would be mild. More likely: *You mean you've forgotten, you damned fool?* Even more likely: *Anyone who can't remember a thing like that doesn't deserve a degree, let alone a passing grade. You're finished!* Boggs, his own adviser. He'd have to remember.

He returned to the phone, picked it up.

". . . so I'd recommend increasing the number of courses you are going to take during the summer but not at any expense to your wife or the child . . ."

He heard a car slowing in front of the building. He put down the phone, went through the apartment, and opened the outer door. A cab was gliding to a stop. He hurried across the sidewalk, removing his wallet as he went. He opened the back door for Ellie, paid the cab driver, helped Ellie out of the car. "Your mother's on the phone," he said. He guided her across the sidewalk, then quickly into the building and to the apartment door. She got to the phone by herself. She lifted the receiver to her ear, held it there for about half a minute, then said, "It's not David, Mother. It's me."

A pause.

"I know, Mother."

A pause.

"Yes, Mother."

A pause.

"I agree, Mother."

He was back in the living room, on his knees, feeling under the chair. If he found the notebook he might find out which writer the paper was supposed to be about. He could worry later about the notes he had missed. He'd lost his syllabus during the second week of the course, but if he wasn't a half-wit he'd at least written the name of the writer in the notebook. His fingers touched something. He pulled it out. The notebook! He flipped the pages. Several with nothing, several with drawings, several more with nothing. He went back to front, found the notes for the second week, what seemed to be the second week. There was a statement:

> Paper due 2 wks after m-term
> *Don't forget!!*

Yes, but when was the midterm? He turned to the page before. Nothing about the midterm. Nothing about the paper. The page after the notation. No mention of writer for paper, paper about writer. No mention of anything.

"He tries, but, no, I honestly can't say he tries very hard."

Pause.

"Yes, Mother."

Pause.

"Yes, Mother."

Pause.

"I intend to, Mother."

He decided the name would come only if he relaxed. He turned around on the floor, reached up, switched on the T.V., sat back in a squat:

A chef who doesn't look like a chef—shirt and tie, hatless—is running from refrigerator to stove, a frying pan full of goo in his hand. The audience laughs. He bangs the frying pan onto one of the burners. Some of the goo spills out onto the stove. More laughter. He looks out at his audience with a grin. "It's also marvelous for cleaning stove stains," he says. Laughter. He picks up something. Says, "Garlic." Starts to peel it, gives up, tosses a couple of lumps of it into pan, the rest on floor. Laughter. Turns to a bowl full of something, reaches in, takes a handful. It looks like onions. Sprinkles some into pan but as many go onto stove. Laughter. Picks up a bottle of wine. Splashes some into pan, onto self, onto stove, onto floor, then takes a swig from the bottle. Extreme laughter. Looks to the side, says, "Good Lord! Already?" Turns to audience. Says, "Time's nearly up. You can figure out the rest by yourself. A little stirring mainly." Slight laughter. "Let's look at the one I started before the show." Picks up hot-pads, hurries to another stove on which sits frying pan. Camera allows last look at pan he's been working with on first stove: the goo is hardening, the mixture is lumpy in many places, much of it cooking over the side. Camera moves to the pan on the second stove. He raises the lid of second pan. "Omelette Henrietta," he says. "Voila!" Ooohs and ahhs. And it *is* beautiful: a smoothly textured surface, evenly colored (in so far as David can make out in black and white), risen nearly to top of pan but none of it spilling over. He dips spoon into it, takes a small bite and says, "Mmm. Heavenly!" The audience coos.

Jesus, David thought, *what a genius, from that* (he remembered the lumpy mess) *to this* (he was looking at the finished omelette). He turned away from the T.V. His eyes landed on the pile of books in front of the big chair. *It's possible*, he thought, *I can make it work the way he made his eggs work. Can, can, can, can, can . . .*

"David?"

He turned.

She was standing in the doorway, legs astraddle, hand against door jamb, stomach sticking obscenely out under faded green frock. Her mouth was sour, her pained eyes hanging a frown. "Mother says you were unresponsive when she spoke to you."

Was responsive, he thought. *Wanted to stuff the receiver down her throat! Pictured her face in the toilet bowl when I pissed! Imagined slamming one of my books closed on her little finger!* He smothered his thoughts. "I heard every word she said," he lied.

"Well then, when are you?"

"When am I what?"

"Going to add some courses and go to the placement office and fill out the forms for a job in the fall and start your thesis and write to colleges which are employing people and ask for an extra section of freshman composition to teach so we'll have moving money and . . ."

"Tomorrow," he said. *James!*

"Tomorrow? I thought tomorrow you had to study for that exam."

He nodded absently.

James it was. On a novel by James. Maybe on some stories. One or the other. It was coming back. A little more thought and he'd . . .

"Well?"

"Well what?"

"When are you?"

What a horrid-looking woman! Who is she? And what does she mean, saying, when are you? When am I what? When am I who?

When am I where? When am I how? When am I when?

"Are you going to tell me or aren't you?"

Mind in parts and pieces. Hearts and theses. Farts and feces. A paper. On Henry James. Who wrote a hundred books at least. And I have read one of the novels. And some short stories, none of which I can . . .

"I want you to answer me, David. When?"

God! Anything. "Next Thursday."

It must have been right, possible, for she turned, clippety-clopped to the kitchen, opened the refrigerator, removed something and went clop, clop, clop into the bedroom.

He looked at the empty doorway. *Next Thursday,* he thought. *Whatever it is, it's next Thursday and I must remember.*

She began chewing.

He stuck his forefingers in his ears.

A paper, and when is it due and the midterm and who would have notes and which ones are missing and suppose it's too late and what is Thursday all about that I have to remember and . . .

Kathy didn't come to his office or leave him new poems. One morning, between classes, he anxiously picked up the phone on the wall near his desk, called information, got her number and dialed it.

"Hullo," said a tired voice that could have been male or female.

"Kathy?" He wasn't sure.

"She's out." It wasn't Kathy, but this time the person did, at least, seem to be a female. Probably her roommate.

"This is David McGrath. Do you know if she's planning to drop by my office soon?"

"David who?"

"McGrath. Maybe she's mentioned me."

"She hasn't mentioned you. She went out of town. She goes away a lot. I dunno when she's coming back. I'll tell her you called."

This roommate was an idiot. She had probably not been paying attention when Kathy talked about him. He hoped that was it.

"She gets a lot of calls."

"Maybe you could write my name down. D-a-v-e M-c-G-r-a-t-h."

A pause. "I wrote it down."

"English Department. I teach here. I'm the one she shows her poems to." He waited, hoping the roommate would give some sign of recognition: *Yeah.* Something.

There was nothing.

"Are you sure she hasn't talked about me?"

"She knows a lot of guys."

"I'm sure she does. I wasn't prying. If you'll just tell her I . . . I'd like to talk to her about several things."

Crunch, crunch, crackety-crack. Was she rubbing the tip of her pencil over the little holes in the mouthpiece? What?

"Hello?"

She was gone.

Nausea turned to diarrhea. He shuffled to the bedroom with bedpan, bulky foods, binding pills. Diarrhea ceased and constipation began. He brought her loosening pills, milk of magnesia, other liquids, Vaseline. The constipation stopped and she began throwing up again.

"Maybe it's the carrots."

"Shut up."

One morning she snapped together like an oyster shell over a giant pearl. He carried her to the car, drove her to university hospital, carried her in. She stayed with her doctor for twenty minutes. She came out upright. On the way home he asked what happened.

"He gave me tranquilizers," she said coldly. "It's probably not physical at all."

He'd never seen a condition so physical. "What then?"

"What do you think?" she said to the windshield.

There were only two kinds of illnesses. It must be the other kind. "Psychological," he said.

Her groan told him nothing.

Psychological. And it had, somehow, to do with him. An old guilt pressed against his back and bent him over the steering wheel.

"I'd like to help," he said before he parked in the alley in back of the apartment. "Give me some idea of what to do."

"Some idea," she repeated.

An hour later she stood in the living room doorway and looked down at him in his chair. "You must be aware," she said.

"What are you talking about?"

"Otherwise you would not have mentioned Mr. Moradaba."

Mr. Moradaba? Were they having assignations after all?

"You see certain things, David. There's no denying it."

She didn't, somehow, seem to be paying him a compliment.

"There must be a connection somewhere."

"I don't know what you're talking about."

She opened one of the bottles her doctor had given her and shuffled to the kitchen for a glass of water. She came back and said, "I don't believe you, David. You *must* know."

Clearly she meant something other than what was in the words themselves. It was important that he figure out what she meant. It was important that he find out without her telling him. A real scholar located even the most obscure books without having to ask the librarian. It was important that he do it like a real scholar, without anyone's help.

"You must."

It was coming to him. It was like one of those subtleties hanging just beneath a James sentence. It had to do with Mr. Moradaba. He was the vague foreshadowing, the whispered clue in the previous chapter. Mr. Moradaba and, of course, he himself, the subject on whom the focus has now shifted. Finally he had it. What she meant was: *Why couldn't he, David, be as sweet and thoughtful as the stranger, Mr. Moradaba?* No. Rather, not quite, for her way, like James's, was oblique. More this: *Since he could recognize in Mr. Moradaba certain loving qualities, why did they not show themselves in him?* That, at least, was closer.

"I . . . I think I understand," he said.

"Do you, David?"

"I think so."

"Then what are you going to do about it?"

A tremendous question. There were surely many answers. Simple answers, complicated answers, answers swimming deeply in his blood. There might eventually be one right answer, or at least the answer she wanted. If so it would take him a while to snare it. For the time being, it was best not to give a partial answer, a wrong answer or any answer that might change tomorrow. He looked up and said, "I'll need a little time, Ellie. I'll have to let you know."

But she wasn't in the doorway. Or in the living room either.

From the bathroom he heard loud grunting noises. The sounds grew louder and more frequent. From one of her apertures something would soon be expelled. He pictured it: wet and misshapen and green.

Ugh!

He got up to close the bathroom door.

She must have been reading his mind, for when he reached the doorway, her foot rose from where she was kneeling in front of the toilet and came quickly backwards, catching the edge of the door, swinging it quietly but swiftly shut.

"Ellie?"

She didn't reply.

He'd been sitting in the booth for nearly four hours. No one had talked to him. He'd talked to no one. His cap had fallen under the table. He hadn't bothered to pick it up. *I'll wait five more minutes,* he'd told himself several times.

Finally she entered.

He watched her glide to her stool, sit, turn and, as usual, begin to survey the people at the front.

I'm ready, he thought. *The time has come.*

He got up, walked over, and tapped her on her bare knee.

She turned, gave him an indifferent look.

"Drink," he said. He had meant it to be a question—"Drink?"—but it came out like a command, the kind he'd heard on hard-sell public service commercials: *Pray. Buy. Give.*

"Who the hell are *you*?" she said.

"David M. McGraff." He turned unsteadily and pointed. "I usually sit in that boof."

She glanced at the booth, seemed to remember, looked at him. "So?"

Her golden silky dress clung to her all the way down to where it stopped about a foot-and-a-half above her knees. Her legs were crossed, themselves like two vivacious women embracing.

"I would like to sit down wif you," he said. He heard his blurred words but couldn't do anything about them.

"For what?"

For what? In the booth he'd thought of many things to say, but now he had no answer. "It's a good question," he said. In fact, he wanted to do more than sit down beside her. The difficulty was saying what he really wanted. "I . . . I want to be wif you." That wasn't it either.

She was looking him up and down. He might have been a door or the side of a truck.

"Well . . . well, I'll tell you." He saw her moving from side to side, falling in and out of focus. He put out his hand to hold her still. The hand landed on her shoulder.

She ignored it, picked up her fancy pink drink, and took a sip.

He floated closer. Their eyes were but an inch apart. He'd get to the point, be direct. That, he decided, was what she wanted him to be. The words came. He spoke into her nostrils. "I . . . I want to fuck you," he said.

She put down her drink and calmly removed his hand, causing him to fall lightly against her. She pressed him back, then straightened, her breasts ascending as if to speak. He felt her hand under his chin. What was she doing? He saw the other hand rise. He closed his eyes, certain she was going to reach back, make a fist and punch him. He waited. She didn't hit him. He opened his eyes.

She was still eyeing him, cool, not angry. "Talk to me when you're sober," she said, removing her hand from his chin.

"I . . . I'm not as drunk as I seem," he said, hopeful.

"You're drunk," she said. "Come back when you're sober."

"All right," he said, seeing she meant it. "Will you, then I mean, will you . . ."

She wouldn't fill in his words. She stared at him until he turned and went back to his booth.

Later, walking home, the chilly air flushed his brain and he calculated the evening. He'd had too much to drink. He had lost his cap. But she hadn't said no. She hadn't said no and he would return. *I don't care about my cap,* he thought.

As he neared the apartment, he had his longest thought of the evening: *Sex is a mystical thing, a most strange and mystical thing.* At the front stairs he cast the thought off as blind, puerile and wordy, the thought of an impractical romantic. He'd be a realist. What had to be done would be done. He turned the key in the door.

On the night before his test she got very sick. She twisted and rolled on the bed. Each time she rolled his head sprang up from the pillow.

"Rrrrouuuppp!"

"Want me to help you to the bathroom?"

"Nuhh . . . rrrhouuuppp!"

It had started in the afternoon, had kept on steadily, increasing in the evening. He'd been cramming for the exam. The more he'd tried to concentrate, the louder she had seemed, the less he'd concentrated. He confused Kurtz's qualities with Marlowe's in *Heart of Darkness.* Absently he'd written on a blank notebook page, *Tess, the Obscure.* And James's sentences, which never seemed to end, were today actually not ending. Neither she nor he had had supper though she'd chewed a few carrots before getting into bed, and he'd had hot chocolate. He'd planned to stay in the living room reading but should have guessed her going to bed wouldn't stop the noises. After looking down and noticing the book that had been on his lap for nearly a half-hour was upside down, he decided to call it quits and go to bed. He'd get up early and study.

But it went on all night:

"Rrrouuuppp!"

Would he have slept had it not gone on? He told himself no, he wouldn't have. He'd have worried about the exam. But would he have gotten up and studied? No. It would have been just the same. He'd have been too nervous to study. *So it's not her fault that I'm not studying?* he asked. *That's right,* he answered, *it's my own fault.*

She, her sickness, has nothing to do with it. He did not believe any of these things but he persuaded himself he did. That way he was able to stop wanting to stand on the bed and jump up and down and stomp her to death. The truth lay safely hidden in some unreachable place beneath his rationalizations.

It wasn't until the next morning when, aching with hunger, he was scraping his eggs off the frying pan that she let go:

"Braggghhhhh. . . . Daaaa-*vid*!"

He dropped the spatula and ran.

She was struggling to get her second leg off the bed. "I'll never make it."

He got his arms under her shoulders and raised her.

Too late. She erupted into the closet, getting his newest pair of shoes. She turned her head and it flowed onto the carpet. He thrust her into the hall. She twisted her head in agony, this way, that; it caught both walls. He pushed her into the bathroom.

"Put me down."

"Where?"

"In there."

"There?"

"Thpphh." She pointed to the tub.

He slid her toward it. As he laid her in she did it again. He struggled to get her mouth over the drain. When he got it there, she'd finished.

"I'll pull out the plug," he said. "For later."

Her hair was wet and frazzled, her head was hanging over her chest, her arms were limp—an old beggar woman, drunk.

He went to the kitchen. He couldn't eat. He thought of the exam. He wasn't ready for the exam. She needed him.

He returned to the bathroom and said he'd stay home.

"Go," she said, not looking up.

He waited.

That was all she said, all she was going to say.

He got to the exam late. He had to borrow a pen. Thoughts came in shotgun blasts. He did his best to put them together, struggled to untangle names, places, books. He remembered a title or two, a significant fact or two. He wrote. What he wrote made no sense. He wrote again. Better. At last a sentence that might get him started: "One must, of course, remember, that Hardy wrote on the heels of the Industrial Revolution when beliefs in the old moralities were beginning to wane." He stared at the sentence. Heels as opposed to head? Heh. No, heels meaning the villains, like . . . Heh heh heh. Now what had he really meant? He read, reread, remembered what he'd intended, forgot, reread, remembered, continued writing. His thoughts began to circle themselves. They were interrupted by thoughts of Ellie. She'd fall asleep. Her head would hit the faucet. She'd knock herself unconscious. The water would be on. Her heel would plug the drain. She'd drown. "Uhhhhgod," he muttered. Boggs, at the front of the room, took the utterance as a sign of intellectual struggle, verification that he'd made up a tough exam, the kind he liked to make up. He looked at David and smiled. It was a "keep plugging" smile. David didn't smile back. He saw Ellie floating through the apartment door. Moradaba would open his door to see where the water was coming from. ("Great Heavens! Thee village ees flooding!") He'd open their door. Ellie, a corpse, would float past. ("Oh my goodness!") Moradaba would grab her, not knowing it was too late. ("I shall save you, Meesus Mogroth!") David's eyes were painfully closed. He'd forgotten where he was in the exam. *I've got to finish*, he thought, opening his eyes to the back of the head of the student in front of him. Where was he? *Hardy and Conrad and . . . Keep going*, he warned himself. He did. He wrote for another hour. He was nearly the last to finish. There were blank spaces throughout his blue book. He didn't go back and fill them in, as planned. He drew arrows from one paragraph through the blank spaces to the next. *Let Boggs's eyes slide down the arrows, let his brain fill in the rest. Let him realize that in silence there is pain. Let him know, sympathize and understand.* He brought the exam to the front of the room. *What bullshit that is*, he thought as he laid the exam on the desk. *Don't need sympathy and understanding. Need something else.* He left the room and hurried to the parking lot. *A reason*, he thought.

He parked the Volkswagen half-on and half-off the sidewalk in front of the apartment and rushed up the stairs to find Mr. Moradaba was standing at their apartment door.

"Meester Mogroth!" he said. "I . . . I was knocking to see whether or not Meesus Mogroth, and you also of course, would care to join me for tea on Fridee afternoon. I have knocked several times. There has, however, been no answer."

She's probably dead, thought David, brushing past him, pushing open the door.

"I'm sorry about thee informality of thee inveetation."

David closed the door, took a step, stepped back, opened the door again. "Tea will be fine. On Friday. I may not make it. I trust she will."

"Excellent. I was thinking of perhaps three, but if eet would be more convenient for her to come later, or, for that matter . . ." He was peering past David, into the apartment, ". . . earlier . . ."

"Tea at three," said David abruptly. "I'll tell her." He closed the door.

Comes thousands of miles, David thought on the way to the bedroom, *all the way from Calcutta. Has no reason to care. But cares.*

"Ellie?"

Not there.

He went to the kitchen.

Not there either.

He's probably still outside, he thought, heading for the bathroom, *listening, caring.*

Door closed. But from behind it, through it, came a smell, the smell of sickness, the smell that seemed to have haunted the place from the beginning.

"Ellie?"

No answer.

Dead!

No!

But could be!

Moradaba, the Concerned. He would go back to the door, say, *Enter the bathroom. See if she's dead or alive. Whatever she is, be a friend and clean away the smell. Then remove her. If she's dead, feel free to make the necessary arrangements. I'll be at the coffee shop on the corner.*

What demon is feeding me such thoughts?

He blocked up his nostrils from the back, breathed through his mouth and pushed open the bathroom door.

In the tub. Head down. Eyes closed. Arms still hanging over sides.

"Ellie?"

She stirred.

Thank goodness. "I'm back."

One eye has opened, only slightly. "Ruh . . . Roger?" An old boy friend.

"Not Roger. Me."

The eye went shut.

"Ellie?"

Eye appeared once more, twisting up from beneath lid, finding, recognizing. "You," she said flatly. The lid held for a second, fell.

There were splashes of orange and brown on bottom of her robe and gown.

"I'll help you out."

"I'm too weak to move."

"Nonsense. You have to get out."

He tried. Arms under shoulders. Hands under butt. One arm under one shoulder, one hand under one half of butt. And so on. She groaned, trying to help. He couldn't get her up.

Will find a saw, a knife, a grinder, he thought. *Take her apart limb by limb. Turn on the water full-blast. Chop her and mince her and send her down the drain. Go to front door and tell Moradaba, My wife has disappeared. Call the police.*

These are someone else's thoughts, he thought, *not mine.*

He looked down at her.

"How am I going to get out, David?"

He looked at tub, door, toilet, her. "Wait," he said.

He ran through the apartment and out the front door. Moradaba would help him get her out. But Moradaba was gone.

Moradaba was not there and his door was closed. David leaped across, hammered on the door. No answer. He hesitated, then turned, ran down the stairs, crossed the sidewalk, opened the Volkswagen trunk and got the tow rope that had been there since they bought the car. He hurried back.

Ellie, wide awake now, looked up, alarmed. "Unhhh?" Was he going to hang her?

He swung the end of the rope under her legs.

He made a lasso, slipped the rope under her hips, raised the rest of the rope up her back and toward her shoulders.

"I'm not an animal, David."

He looped the rope under her shoulders and knotted it behind. "Hold the sides of the tub," he said, "and try to raise yourself."

"I'm too weak."

"Try."

She tried but could do nothing.

He braced himself against the side of the tub and pulled. She rose a little. He got to the toilet, braced himself, pulled. She was coming out. He got to the door jamb and braced himself. She had reached the edge, was hovering, about to flop back in or go to the floor.

"Get your legs over."

"My legs are numb."

"All right. Balance there. I'm going to let go."

She balanced.

He let go. He rushed forward, arms extended. She was tottering when he hit her. The two of them almost went back into the tub, didn't. Half standing, he hung onto her around the chest. She swayed this way, then that, then held steady. He eased her back. His legs bent a little, a little more. Together, steadily, slowly, they went to the floor.

He dragged her back into the room. He helped raise her to her feet. He guided her onto the bed. He looked at her stomach. *It's not my child*, he thought, *I could not have done that. She was raped by a hippopotamus.*

"How are you doing?" he said.

She wheezed.

He stood above her. There was one thing he wanted to say. He said it: "I'm sure I flunked the exam."

"What do I, puff, care about your exam?"

"Do you want anything?"

"Yes. Go away."

He left the bedroom. He cleaned the house. The job took nearly two hours. Several times he opened the bedroom door to see that she was all right. When she was asleep he tiptoed in and cleaned the bedroom quietly. He found more than a dozen carrot stubs. He took them on a plate to the kitchen and let them roll off, like little heads, into the garbage can.

In his department mailbox he found an envelope, peach-colored, vaguely perfumed, unsealed, no name or address. He tore it open, recognized the scratchy handwriting, read:

Dave—

Am cutting out. Have had it up to here with that god damn university, etc. Am going to N.Y.C. with a friend to write and find a job and wish you were the one. We could have started a beautiful thing but I knew that day I was last in your office you wouldn't be able to, maybe ever.

It's all a game and I don't think you know it. I don't believe you really care about that fat lady you mentioned, just think you do. It was the way you stood stiff by the window and the tightness in your voice and other shit I probly will only get down in my poems someday. Like maybe I was just a year or two too late for you. Don't know, will try to find out when I write about you. What I know is you live in an old world and bullshit yourself hanging on to what you don't want and if it isn't that fat lady it will be someone else. I have enough problems without taking on yours, not that you asked me to, but I mean I don't have a hundred pounds of guilt to deliver to the fucking oppressors of this world before finding what I have to find. I wanted to see you and was there when you called but told my roomate not to say so because by then I knew you would be poison in my soup. If you had come by my place and said "let's go" and I had seen something different in your face or the way you stood there or something I probly would have gone. Too late, man. Too late. I hope you learn how to swim for yourself but don't think you will. I am going places without you but won't forget.

Kathy

P.S. Will be gone when you get this.

He shoved the rest of his mail back into his mailbox and rushed to his office. He opened the drawer where he'd put her poems. He'd planned to read them aloud to her. No, had planned to have her read them aloud to him. But she hadn't come by and now he fumbled about under some memos he'd stuffed in the drawer until he found them. He sent his finger in—like picking a card out of a deck—removed one and read:

Invent Me

Let your tongue fall
To a beginning, my seed,
Pomegranate,
Sweetly warm, sweetly wet,
Rolling between your lips,
Against your tongue.
Let it grow til you crush it,
Spill it warmly to your wishes . . .

The poem fell from his hand back into the drawer. He looked at it, thinking he might pick it up, didn't. He'd send his hand down again, find another poem, a less direct poem, would work his way back to the one he had started, would do that because it, the one he'd plucked out, was too . . . too electrifying to read first. Yes, that's what he'd do. No. Couldn't. They'd all in one way or another give him shocks and tremors the way the first one had. Why hadn't he read them before? He hadn't read them because it had been she, not her poetry, that had interested him. But she was in the poems, speaking to him, even waiting, and he would have known that had he . . . But he hadn't.

He shuffled to the window. The note was a trick. She'd had to do something to wake him up. That's why she'd sent it. He looked down at the sidewalk where he'd seen her last. She'd appear in a moment, stand below him, her soft hair twisting to hold itself against the breeze, her hands confidently on her hips, her eyes speaking up to him: *Well, I'm waiting. Are you coming with me or aren't you?* Classes were changing. There were many students on the sidewalk. He looked to the right, toward the administration building, then to the left, toward the science building. She wasn't among the students.

No one, in fact, was looking up.

He ordered a beer and went to the men's room. He came back to find her standing beside his stool, watching him cold-eyed. "You may as well come over and buy me a drink," she said.

He did.

He sat beside her, trying to find things to say. He couldn't. *This is all happening too fast*, he thought.

She wasn't looking at him.

He said, "I think about you all the time."

She didn't seem to care.

He said, "I hope I didn't alarm you with anything I said last time."

She didn't even seem to hear that.

He said, "It's not just that I'm horny. There's something about the way you look and walk and . . ."

She turned to him and said, "Stop talking. I like what you like as much as you. Don't make a big thing of this. If there was someone better around, I'd be drinking with him."

"I . . . I see," he said, grateful for these clues.

"If you want to have your kicks, stop giving me a line of shit. I don't need one. In fact, don't talk at all. Just try to pretend you're a real lover, which I'm sure you're not. Show me something more than your nervousness."

He would, or would try to. He put his hand on her thigh. She didn't shove it away, so he slid it upward. She closed her eyes. He pressed his face close to hers. He began to get hard. She took his hand and moved it to her other thigh. He felt himself harder. "I've got to have you," he said.

"Shut up," she said.

He did. He moved his hand slowly down her thigh. He heard a groan of satisfaction. He pulled his stool close to hers, her breast against his upper arm. He turned and kissed her, sending his tongue into her mouth. She rolled her tongue around his, then eased away. "Let's go," she said, getting up.

He followed her to the door.

Too fast, he thought on the way out. *Maybe I can't do it.*

She reached back, took his hand, led him down the sidewalk.

Must and will, he thought, watching her thighs moving under the streetlights.

They went through a dark entrance-way and up some creaky stairs. There was a door at the top. She used the dim light from the street to find her key and open the door.

A light went on inside.

Colors assaulted him. There were paintings hung all about. The wall itself was bright orange. The faces in the paintings were tortured faces and the colors were black and blood-red and that bright orange again. One painting, especially, caught his eye. It hung near the center of the back wall: an ugly woman, half-clothed, her torso bared to the viewer, her face decades older than her soft pink belly, her expression full of rage and insult. He turned away quickly.

"Sit down." She pointed to the sofa.

He went over, sat down.

She loosened her belt. The bright print dress, more a kimono, fell a bit, then parted between her breasts. She twisted her head from side to side and her hair fell in a shower of fire. She moved her feet slowly apart, opening the dress, freeing her breasts to billow whitely above her tapered torso. She moved forward and sat down beside him. She kicked away her sandals and pulled her bare legs onto the sofa. She leaned back against the sofa arm. Her thighs seemed to spread.

He sat very still beside her, worried that this had become part of a trick, a tantalizing trick: when he responded she would stop. The least of his fantasies rarely worked out. What was happening exceeded the best. How could it continue?

"Touch me," she said.

He lowered his eyes, saw that she was naked below. He reached carefully down, forefinger out, and entered the slice. It was oily. He pushed in, went down, deeper.

Her head had fallen back, and she was groaning.

He turned his finger, then brought it slowly out. "I have never done anything like this to a stranger," he said.

"Don't stop," she said.

He slid his finger in and out with a steady rhythm.

"Lick me," she said.

Oh, God! He'd dreamed of certain women wanting such things but had decided long ago that they didn't exist. Maybe he'd been wrong. Maybe all the women he'd desired had been waiting for this. If so, the losses were countless.

"Lick!"

He slipped off the sofa, onto the floor. He turned one of her legs out, pressed his face down, extended his tongue.

He'd go in. He began to fumble with the belt on his pants. He'd go in and stay in. Fumble fumble. Afterwards, he'd come here and live with her, as a lover, husband, a servant, clean-up boy, whatever it took. The belt was nearly off.

A sound.

He sat up.

"Don't stop," she said.

No other Volksagen in America ticked like that. He leaped up, dove half way over the sofa back, pulled the curtain aside.

"What are you doing?"

The car slowed into a parking place between Margaret's door and the Amazon's stairway. He saw Ellie's puzzled face against the windshield, peering out into the night. He pulled back from the window, said, "I'm doomed."

"What are you talking about?"

"Does Margaret know where you live?"

"Of course."

Ellie was coming after him. Margaret would tell her he'd gone out with the Amazon, then tell her where she lived. "Where's your back door?"

"What are you talking about?" The Amazon sat up, turned, pulled the curtain back. "Who's out there?"

"My wife."

"Wife!" It was like a bark. "You didn't say you had a wife! You don't have a ring on! What do you mean, wife?" She snapped her kimono closed, stood up, glanced at the window, looked down at him. "You're cheating on your wife?"

"Cuh . . . calm down." He gestured her to sit but she didn't. "Just tell me where your back door is and we'll be all right."

"I don't have a back door."

"Oh shit."

Crickety-plonk, crickety-plonk.

The Amazon was squatting, picking up her sandals. "You're a fucking cheat!"

Crickety-plonk, crickety-plonk.

"Oh shit."

The Amazon looked to the door. "What's that noise?"

Crick-ett-tee plonk. Cri-kett . . . tee.

"Listen," he whispered. "She seems to be slowing down or . . . or stopping."

Plonk-crickety.

"Why is she walking like that?" the Amazon asked.

Plonk-crickety.

"I . . . I think she's going back down."

Plonk-crickety.

"Answer me! Why?"

He didn't answer.

She went to the window and looked out. "Jesus Christ! She's pregnant!"

"Keep quiet. It's not as if . . ."

But the sentence wouldn't be completed. The Amazon knew all she had to know and was doing what she had to do: kicking him. He was on his hands and knees and she was kicking him toward the door. "Get out of here you murdering pig-bastard!"

"I don't feel evil," he said, wincing against her blows. "I'm not happy but, nnhh, I don't feel evil!"

"Go home and (kick kick) take care of your crippled wife, you (kick kick) son-of-a-bitch!"

What was happening? Why was she kicking him? Who had he offended? Wouldn't he be happier with Ellie after a night with her? So what injury to Ellie?

Kick!

"Nnnhh!"

"Get out!"

None. The opposite. He'd be gentler, more informed, better, happier. Ellie, too, would be happier. He'd learn from the Amazon and take his lessons home.

Whack! Whack!

The Amazon was trying to slam the door but his legs were in the way.

He turned, looked up at her. "I am what I am. And *where.* I mean here. I wanted to fuck you! I still do! Give me a chance! Give my wife a chance!"

She brought her foot back and delivered it into his ass, popping him onto the landing.

The door slammed behind him.

"Out of what wisdom shaping what morality does this change arise!" he shouted at the closed door.

She didn't answer.

"You won't fuck me! But at least answer me!"

"Anyone who married you ought to be a cripple!" she shouted from the other side. "You're a monster!"

He stood painfully and looked down. He'd seen Richard Widmark in a movie of childhood or adolescence, pushing an old lady in a wheelchair down a flight of stairs. He'd send himself tumbling down these steep and narrow stairs. He'd do it to make up for what Richard Widmark had done to the old lady. Boombedy boombedy boombedy clomp! To make up for an actor in a movie? To make up for what hadn't happened but had only seemed to happen? To make up for having accidentally been there, for having accidentally seen what had only seemed to happen?

No.

Something else.

He'd do it to make up for real things. To make up for what he'd done and hadn't done to Ellie. To make up for what he'd done and hadn't done to everyone, for what other people did to each other, to make up for their crimes, for all the crimes of the human race, not just present crimes but crimes before and ever after. To make up for . . .

The hell with it.

He got up and hobbled down the stairs.

"Ellie?"

No answer.

He'd limped home, bruised from the Amazon's kicks, heavy in his bones. The car hadn't been parked in front. He'd gone around to the back and checked the alley. It hadn't been there either. He'd run up the back stairs, entered the apartment, called, gotten no answer. Now, nearly breathless, he was rushing from kitchen to bathroom to bedroom, rushing and calling.

Not a sound, not a stir.

He stumbled back to the living room. *She's out there, still looking,* he told himself. *She'll be back soon. No need to panic.* On the Amazon's stairs she'd decided he was not up there. Then she'd gone back to the car and driven about looking for him. Why? He didn't know. There were other things he didn't know. Had the car been parked in front when he left the Amazon's? Had she waited to see if he'd come out? Had she been watching him? He hadn't thought to look. The notion was ridiculous anyway. She'd probably left right away, gone searching for him, was still searching—his office, the library, the hamburger place. She'd soon return.

Something is catching up with me, he thought, eyeing the sofa, feeling his heaviness. His eyes closed. He pictured himself on a soft path somewhere, looking back in darkness, seeing the outlines of an animal, a large animal. The animal had golden glistening eyes and seemed to be moving, moving forward, moving toward him . . . He opened his eyes. He was swaying. His knees were going soft. *Something. Must rest.* He took a step toward the sofa but tripped on a book and toppled onto the pile. He felt the sharp edges of books pressing up against his torso and legs. He was too exhausted to raise himself. Instead, he wiggled into the books until he could no longer feel the sharp edges. *Something,* he thought, searching the darkness behind his lids. He waited, saw himself once more, peering backwards. *A tiger or maybe a panther.* He watched himself watching, waiting to see the golden glistening eyes. This time he couldn't see them.

He awakened to sounds. Cars: straining to start, growling along the street in front of the apartment, screeching to stop. He raised his head, looked toward the front door: morning light pressed against the opaque glass. He heard the tippety-tap of footsteps in the apartment above. He pulled himself up.

"Ellie?"

No reply.

Jesus!

Hands out, balancing himself against walls, he scrambled from room to room, this time looking under and behind things, beginning to panic, searching for a toe, an ear, a trickle of blood, anything. He noticed for the first time that the bedroom was more than its usual mess: several drawers open, clothes flung about, shoes stirred up in the closet. Had it been that way last night? Had he missed it?

He staggered to the kitchen. Maybe she'd tried to drive to her mother's place. But why hadn't she called from there? He pictured her trapped behind the Volkswagen wheel in a ditch, somewhere between here and Central Liberty. One frightened thought delivered another: she hadn't left town at all, had been beaten, robbed, and raped in one of those alleys around Margaret's. And another: she'd cracked up and done something terrible, like driven to the front lawn of the mayor or the college president, gotten out and stood there wailing out her complaints until they came and locked her up.

He was making coffee now, trying to calm himself. He wasn't succeeding. *Whatever it is,* he thought, *it's as bad as any of these things.*

The phone rang.

The coffeepot dropped from his hands and splashed to the floor so that he had to leap back to keep from being scalded. He rushed to the phone, picked it up.

"I want to speak to Eleanor." It was Mrs. Tanner. That meant she wasn't at her mother's.

What could he say? He couldn't tell Mrs. Tanner she was in a ditch, an alley, an asylum. He couldn't say he didn't know.

"Where is she?"

"In . . . bed," he said, trying to sound calm, "sleeping peacefully."

"She wasn't feeling well last night. She asked me to call this morning. She said she'd be awake."

"She's not. She's sleeping, finally. I don't want to wake her."

A pause, then, "I'll call back. In the meantime I may as well share with you a few useful insights I've had regarding . . ."

He raised the receiver above his head, thinking to smash it against something. He looked about. There was nothing to smash it against, nothing that would break it, stop her sounds. Just as well. Unresponsive last time, she'd said. Nothing but trouble from Ellie if he smashed the phone. Slowly he lowered the receiver. He'd hang on, at least for a few minutes.

". . . and though Herbert's condition resulted from a disease over which, for the short period during which he suffered from it, he had no control, the symptoms, particularly as they showed themselves to me and to others around him, were not unlike yours."

His eyes were tightly, painfully, closed. Ellie had told him about her father's problem. He knew what her mother was referring to. "I am not an alcoholic, Mrs. Tanner."

"No matter. The effects are the same and, for that reason, I am certain you need pity more than scorn which is why I am not castigating you. I do, however, want you to know that at no time did he treat me as badly as you have treated Eleanor, which is probably why I was able to save my wits and see to the management of the farm. For one thing, he did not carouse during the evening, as I understand you have been doing, did not make fun of my ailments, not that I had many, and did not close his heart or even his mind to my most basic needs. Oh, there were indeed crises for me. I know what I went through that Christmas when, I'm ashamed to say, he followed Eleanor's cousin, Helga, around like a common hound. But that was temporary, Mr. McGrath, a symptom of his deeper troubles. It was after those holidays that he began to come to his senses, in fact."

He wouldn't, couldn't, put up with another second of this. Whether he seemed unresponsive or not, he'd have to hang up. "Mrs. Tanner, I . . ."

"Just a moment. I want you to know that when Herbert got to the root of his condition, things began to change. By April of the year following that terrible Christmas, he was on his tractor supervising the work in the fields."

"Mrs. Tanner?"

"Indeed, we began to work it out together by speaking to each other. By relying on our pastor and others, by realizing that in the farm, in our children, we shared a certain commonality of interests which . . ."

"I am terribly constipated, Mrs. Tanner, and am bending with pain." He actually bent over as if to demonstrate for her and, as he bent, actually did feel pain. As he began to straighten, he looked into the kitchen and saw Eleanor's green pumps, her best shoes, under the kitchen table, standing in a puddle of coffee. *What are they doing there?* He straightened. The pain he'd invented was real now, had invaded his intestines.

". . . and she's a woman who knows what she wants, Mr. McGrath. She will not, I warn you, put up with . . ."

"Must go. Emergency. Goodby." Click.

Shoes might mean other things taken out. He went into the bedroom, could not tell by looking at the clothes strewn about what had been taken, what had not. *This is an emergency,* he thought.

He was at the phone. His finger was quivering. It took him several tries to get it in the hole labelled "O." Finally he did, turned it all the way. The ringing began. There were other sounds, a whistling sound from outside, the kitchen window rattling.

Finally: "Operator."

"Police," he replied.

Interminable clicking, then: "Central Station. Go ahead."

"My wife . . . has disappeared."

"Just a moment. Who's speaking?"

"McGrath. David. Fifty . . . fifty . . . fifty-oh-one Jefferson."

"Calm down, Buddy. What's this wife of yours look like?"

"Brown. Hair is brown. She's two years younger than me. No, three. Has a blue or green coat. She's about . . ."

"Hey! Slow down. Where did you lose her?"

"I was in an apartment, . . . a, a friend's. I looked out the window . . ."

"Where's this apartment?"

"On . . . on Market Street, near Margaret's Tavern and . . . wait. I forgot to tell you something. I forgot to tell you she's pregnant."

"Christ sake! How long has she been pregnant?"

"I . . . We aren't sure. Pretty long."

"Did you call the hospital?"

"Hospital?"

"Maybe she went there to have her kid."

"Do you think . . .?"

"That's what happens, buddy."

He dropped the phone. He ran into the kitchen. He ran back to the phone. Why was he running? He picked up the phone, pressed the button, dialed "0" again, waited, got the operator, asked for the university hospital number, got it, hung up, dialed, waited again, got the hospital, asked for the maternity ward, waited again, heard a voice, panted, "I'm Mr. McGrath. My wife . . ."

"Your wife is resting." The voice was indifferent.

"Did she . . . did she . . .?"

"She's had a child." Even colder. "The child is well."

He could think of nothing else to ask.

"I'll . . . I'll . . . I'll be there."

He dropped the phone, ran once more into the kitchen. Pain fluttered through muscles and bones. He heard the whistling sounds from outside. He looked about. *I am in the kitchen*, he realized. He turned, started out, stopped. He'd seen something at the center of the table.

He picked it up.

Why didn't I notice this before?

He held it, staring at it.

It was here all the time.

He dropped it and ran toward the apartment door.

Warning winds rose out of Kansas, Oklahoma, Missouri, swept across the farm fields south of town, were now spinning over streets and sidewalks, twisting toward the river, then breaking across, raging into the hills on the other side.

Small branches, ripped mercilessly from larger ones, lay broken before him. Running, he stumbled once and fell forward, but threw his hands out, kept his balance. In his legs the pain churned. He slowed to a trot, passed a store window, saw his raincoat flapping behind him like a broken sail. He picked up speed as he reached the last of the campus buildings, was running again when he turned down the street leading to the bridge.

Why hadn't he found the note last night? He'd been in and out of the kitchen several times, last night and this morning. It had screamed up at him and he should have seen it:

> David,
>
> I searched for you and couldn't find you. Am not surprised. Have been without you all along. The labor started and has now stopped but will start again. Am going to the hospital alone. Don't bother coming. I don't want to see you.
>
> E.

It wasn't too late. He'd say, *Things that are visible, Ellie, are not always seeable.* No. He wouldn't say that. She'd mock him for that. But he *would* say, would *have* to say, something.

He reached the bridge. The wind lashed at him from this side, then that. He gripped the steel railing for support. He looked down as he moved. The water was murky and dark. It whipped against the pilings, and he thought he felt the bridge quivering. He looked down again. The water seemed depthless. He didn't like looking at it. He rushed to the other side, stopped, glanced down the empty highway, then started across it, toward the sidewalk that led up the hill to the hospital.

The strain of labor had been too much. She'd written the note in anger. But now the baby was safely born and she'd probably forgotten she'd written it. She'd be concerned about, would ask him about, other things.

What other things?

Possibly the Red Amazon.

A moment, Ellie, only a moment. Nothing really happened. It's over now. We can get back to . . .

Someone slammed a window shut. He turned, saw a sign: DISPENSARY. Someone had shut a window to his left, and now all the windows, the ones across the front of the dispensary building, were shut. He turned, hurried on.

He would talk to her. He would talk away her fears and angers. No matter what she said, that would be his approach. There was nothing that couldn't be talked away.

At the top of the hill the wind hit him face-on, was steady, pressing him back as if to push him back down the hill. He saw that across the street, in the parking lot, the cars were swaying. No one else was on the sidewalk. He turned, leaned against the wind, moved with much effort down the sidewalk toward the main entrance.

I will say nothing, he thought. *I will enter her room as if nothing unusual has happened, nothing is out of place. She may ask questions. I won't lie. I will answer truthfully, but I will urge her to think of the future, not the past. Something awful has ended in our lives. It's time to think about beginnings.*

The wind worked like a heavy lean-to against the glass door. It took all his weight to get it to budge. Finally, he had to raise his foot to the steel strip beside the door and pull hard with the extra leverage of his leg. The door opened slowly. He twisted into the lobby. The door crashed shut behind him.

A wrinkled woman, not a nurse, stood behind the main desk. He spoke his name, said, "My wife had a baby sometime last night."

The wrinkled woman spoke in a dry voice: "The maternity ward is on the fourth floor. But you musn't go into your wife's room until you've spoken to the nurse in charge." She gave no explanation.

He was alone in the elevator. The wind whistled hollowly through the shaft. The elevator didn't seem to be moving upward at all. But the wind in the shaft was making it shimmy. Maybe it was the wind that was making it go so slowly. Was it going at all? He looked up. On the panel of numbered lights, the 3 went out and the 4 lit up. He waited. He could still not feel any upward movement. At last the door opened. As he stepped from the elevator he felt the warm wind passing downward over him.

A dark-haired young woman sat at a table behind the maternity counter. She was writing something on a chart attached to a clipboard. He made a sound and she looked up, gave him an indifferent look. He spoke his name. She pushed the chart aside slowly and stood, still looking at him. "I'm sorry, Mr. McGrath," she said, "your wife does not want to see you."

He stared at her, then looked past her down the hallway adjoining the counter. His eyes moved back to her. "What do you mean, doesn't want to see me?"

She hesitated, as if uncertain as to whether or not she would answer. Finally she said, "Last night when your wife came in she was very distraught. We had to call a psychiatrist, Dr. Grace. Apparently . . ." the nurse turned away from him now and the gesture added to his growing uneasiness. " . . . apparently she wants to leave you."

"No," he said insistently. "She's been through a lot. We both have." He realized he wasn't speaking only to the nurse but to himself, and, in a way, to Ellie too. "I wasn't around last night and it upset her. I had no idea she was . . ."

"Mr. McGrath," the nurse said firmly, looking at him, "Dr. Grace has spent several hours with her, both before and after your child's birth. He has instructed us not to let you in to see her. He wouldn't do that without good reasons. Apparently she's been on the verge of a breakdown and has, somehow, held herself together until the child was born. But now . . ."

David noticed she was standing between him and the rooms beyond, partly blocking his way. He turned, as if to start back for the elevator, then turned back and bolted around her.

"Mr. McGrath!"

"Ellie!" he shouted, running down the hallway. "Ellie!"

She was propped against a couple of pillows, her eyes barely visible under the lids, her arms loose at her sides. She seemed either about to fall asleep or just to have awakened.

"Ellie?"

She turned slightly, found him.

"I . . . I had to run down the hallway."

"Please, Mr. McGrath."

He turned.

The nurse stood behind him, frowning. "You mustn't stay."

"But this is my wife. I . . ." He turned back to Ellie.

She was looking past him to the nurse. "A few minutes," she said dryly.

He turned once more.

The nurse hesitated, then turned and went back up the hallway.

He looked again at Ellie. All that had so far happened seemed to have nothing to do with her. Now, she watched him with indifferent eyes.

"I'm sorry about last night. I . . . I . . ."

"I don't care about last night," she said flatly.

"But I should have been there when you were ready to go."

"That doesn't matter."

"It *does* matter," he said, taking a step toward her. "Of course it matters. I should have called or . . ."

"It does *not* matter."

Said another way, her words might have reassured him. They did just the opposite. "What do you mean?"

"We're finished," she said calmly, her eyes still on him. "I'm leaving you." Her face tightened a bit and there might have been a sob, the beginning of a cry. But the tears didn't come. "I can't live with you. It's probably been true for some time. I just couldn't admit it until the baby was born."

"No." He felt his legs going soft.

"Yes," she said firmly.

Just after he'd broken from the nurse and before he'd glanced into the first room, he'd heard a metallic sound, the sound of something hitting the floor. It seemed to beckon him. He turned and followed the sound to the room from which it seemed to have come. Somehow he wasn't surprised to look into the room and find Ellie. The air seemed to be full of preparations: the wind, the hospital noises, that sound.

He took a step toward the bed. His legs had become very weak and he felt himself sinking. "I want . . . I want to . . ." He reached out, caught the side of the mattress to keep himself from going all the way down.

"You don't understand," she said coldly, certainly. "You'll probably never understand."

"Ellie," he said weakly.

"I want you to go now, David."

His legs lost their strength. He went to the floor, landed on something jagged. He reached down, found the object and raised it: a set of keys, on a ring, her keys, the keys to the car.

"Take the car. Go away. Find someone else."

"Ellie," he said, raising himself.

"Go."

"No. You . . . you're not yourself. You've been through a lot and . . ."

Her hand, a fist, was squeezed tightly around the switch that hung from the cord above the bed, her thumb pressed against the button on the switch.

"Don't," he whispered.

Her eyes didn't reach past an invisible point in the air between them. "Go away," she said. "You must go away. Now!"

"Why are you talking to me like that?" he pleaded, not hearing the footsteps behind him.

She didn't answer.

Strong arms were clamped onto his shoulders. He felt himself being pulled away from the bed. He saw white trouser legs moving on both sides of his own legs. He saw the bed recede. He caught a glimpse of her face, distant, indifferent, the same as it had been when he came into the room. Now he was in the hallway and felt himself being raised, then pushed up the hallway.

He was at the counter.

"I'm sorry, Mr. McGrath." It was the dark-haired nurse, standing before him. "We have no choice." She paused, then said, "Dr. Grace says you can see the baby before you go. One of the orderlies will accompany you."

"My wife," he said.

"This is Dr. Grace's number," she said, handing him a sheet of paper. "I think he'd like you to call him."

He wanted, suddenly, to reach out and slide his hands up over her narrow torso to where her breasts came sharply out.

One of the orderlies released him. The other held on and said, "Let's go."

He'd touch her and she'd lead him to an empty room. They'd bare themselves to each other. They'd climb into a bed. They'd lock themselves to each other. They'd remain for a long time.

"One of the orderlies will stay here," she said, "in case you attempt to return."

"I want to stay," he said. "For a few minutes. And talk to you."

"No." She gave him a troubled look. "You must leave now. It's important. You don't know how serious this is."

"This way," said the second orderly, releasing him, pointing down the hallway on the other side of the counter.

He turned around, wanting to call out to Ellie. But what would he say? He turned back, looked at the orderly's finger, then at the nurse, who watched him urgently.

"C'mon," said the orderly.

There was no choice. He moved slowly past the orderly, around the counter, toward the other hall.

An old nurse held the basket-bed at an angle, tilted forward, as if she were displaying a large photograph or a hat. He viewed the baby carefully but could not, somehow, see anything distinctive in its features. There was a tuft of dark hair, a round chinless face, eyes pinched between skin—dark blue or brown, he couldn't tell—but nothing in the expression that set if off from other babies he'd seen.

He noticed its movements: the tiny arms going in little circles, the head shifting rapidly from side to side, and under the blanket throbbing movements that brought to mind how it had felt when he'd put his hand on Ellie's stomach. As it struggled its eyes seemed to be fixed on him, though the head was constantly moving about. No sound passed through the glass, but he knew it was screaming, screaming and maybe choking. He glanced at the nurse. Strangely, she too seemed troubled. The basket wobbled a bit in her hands. It looked as though she might not be able to hold it much longer. He shook his head abruptly. The nurse read his signal and carefully lowered the basket-bed into its cradle. She seemed grateful to be rid of it.

Moments later, as he followed the orderly to the elevator, he tried to recall at least a detail of the baby's features, something he might remember later, compare to a feature of his own or of Ellie's, or of one of their relatives. But there were only those movements, that color. For all he could recall, it might have been someone else's child. What, then, would he take with him? What then, would he hold in his mind's eye? What, then, would he call back later? A tiny child moving, an infant red and faceless. Nothing more.

They had reached the elevator. He turned to the orderly, intending to ask that they go back, that he be allowed to take another look. Before he could speak the door opened. The orderly extended his hand toward it. David hesitated, then entered.

There was no blast of air when he got into the elevator this time, but once again it didn't seem to be moving. He looked up, waited. Finally the 4 went out and the 3 came on. *Eyes*, he thought, sticking his hands nervously into his jacket pocket. He felt keys in one of them, removed them and looked: the ones he'd fallen on. He didn't remember picking them up. He returned them to his pocket and looked up at the panel of lights: 2. *Will it ever get to the bottom*? He put his hands into the back pockets of his pants, took them out, stuffed them into the front ones, felt paper, pulled it out. It was the sheet with Dr. Grace's number. He held it and looked up at the panel once more. At last the 1 appeared. He waited. Finally the door opened. Now there was a rush of air, passing up from the bottom of the elevator, cold this time. He took a step forward and stopped.

A lot of people were in the lobby, clusters of them, several looking toward the elevator, at him. He stood there, wondering why they'd turned. By the time he realized that the opening of the elevator doors had simply drawn their eyes in his direction—several were turning away now—the doors began to close. He reached out, touched the edge of one door, causing both to snap open. He lowered his eyes and moved out, crossing the lobby, going past one group, around another, toward the entrance.

He heard a man say, "Tore hell out of Morgansburg. It was on the radio." There was a general buzz of conversation. Another man said, "Be bad for the next twenty-four hours, maybe longer." Nurse's aides were distributing coffee and doughnuts. He refused a refreshment, skidded past the last group, pressed his weight against the glass door and went out.

Something about eyes. A trash container was cemented to the ground a few yards from the glass door. He stopped, looked at the sheet of paper with Dr. Grace's number, hesitated, then dropped it in. He sent his eyes across to the parking lot across the street, spotted the Volkswagen and headed toward it.

What?

He maneuvered the car down the winding road at the back of the hill, careful to avoid debris that had fallen or been blown out earlier. Even now the wind was gusting, sending little tremors through the car, flinging leaves and paper before him. About halfway down, near one of the hospital buildings, a garbage can came clanking out of a driveway and rolled toward the car. He had to apply the brake swiftly. He watched the can hurtle past, spewing its contents as it went. He thought an object so big might have been pushed, and he turned back to the driveway to see if someone was standing there; no one was. *The wind*, he assured himself, and he continued toward the highway.

Unwanted thoughts had been whisking through his brain. *Eyes.*

He was thinking about the baby's eyes, recalling how they kept moving away from and then back to him, as if he'd been the one object the infant had been sure of, something fixed, a kind of anchor against its confusion and fright. He'd heard that newborn babies can't see. But maybe they could intuitively sense another's presence. Had the baby been trying to locate him? Had it somehow known this would be their last contact? Had its screams, then, been the violent screams of abandonment? Such questions. How could he know the answers? And why had he remembered the movements, those eyes, but nothing special in the face, not even the color of the eyes?

He'd reached the stop sign at the bottom of the hill. He looked to the left, saw that no cars were approaching on either of the two right lanes. He swung his head to the right. Those lanes were clear too. Instead of releasing the clutch and turning, however, he began to scan the woods on the other side of the highway, part of an uncleared strip of land that narrowed between highway and river as both curved around the hospital hill toward the bridge. Once again he checked the highway—still clear—then shifted into first gear and turned right. He steered from the outer to the inner lane, drove several hundred feet, then slowed, glancing once more into the woods. The river was now visible here and there: pieces of gray ribbon against a black landscape. He checked the rear-view mirror; no cars were approaching from behind. He looked ahead; no cars there, either. He had been slowing steadily, and now he came to a stop. To his left, across the highway, was a dirt access road passing between two clumps of trees. He swung the car quickly around, crossed the two opposite lanes and drove onto the access road.

"Christ, Ellie," he whispered.

He drove forward between the trees and stopped about ten feet from the bank. He'd watched boys fishing here during the summer and knew that the bank, though low, dropped sharply, steeply. He raised the clutch, feeling the touch of giddiness he had sometimes felt coming out of Margaret's after a couple hours of drinking. He thought of pressing the gas pedal down hard and shooting swiftly forward, but he didn't. Instead he applied a steady pressure and moved ahead slowly. In a moment he felt the front wheels sink smoothly into the mud. He braced himself as the car nosed forward, then slid easily down the bank and into the murky water.

He hadn't once thought of suicide, the word or the concept, and now there was a slow exhilaration, as if this descent had more to do with staying alive than with dying. It was a feeling like the feeling he'd had when he'd first approached the Red Amazon, when he'd entered the classroom for Boggs's exam knowing he wasn't prepared, even when he'd awakened this morning to find Ellie still missing. It wasn't a good feeling or a bad feeling, and, though it had come over him infrequently, it was a tangible feeling, maybe indelible, an evidence somehow of continuity, not death.

As the car began to sink, he was aware only of the elements around him: the shiny dials of the dashboard, the black, hard steering wheel, the knuckles of his hands on the wheel and, above all, the overwhelming presence of water: sliding darkly over the windshield, swishing loudly through openings around the dashboard, swirling coldly over his feet. The car, half-submerged, nosed upward for a moment, then began to sink rapidly. The water climbed toward his knees. He saw it pressing against the windows, enclosing the car. The car struck, bounced, and glided. It struck again, bounced a little less, glided. The water moved toward his waist. He felt it laying silt against his skin. The car bounced and glided once more, then settled. The water was raising him from the seat. Soon it would cover him and he would have to take his last breath, hold it until the water forced his mouth open. He rolled to the side, then came upward, floating.

Something was moving. He pulled himself forward, getting his head over the top of the steering wheel, his face against the windshield. Something or someone was passing back and forth, but, because of the muddiness of the river, he couldn't see what it was. Though it was moving from side to side, it seemed also to be getting closer. There were now only inches between the top of the water and the ceiling. He caught his breath, sank under and searched through the water. He saw the gray movements, closer now, even closer. He raised his head and blew the air out. He had to twist his head to the side to get another breath. He did so, then went under and searched again.

He saw it now, a few feet from the windshield: a large, gray, ugly face. It moved toward him, its tiny eyes shifting from side to side, wide sullen lips twisting under long outrising strands. It came closer, closer, and finally touched the windshield. Only the eyes were moving now, still shifting, shifting and searching. Dizzy, uncertain, half-blinded by the dirty water, he couldn't see that the creature was a large catfish. He was delirious now, and, in his confusion, he reached out to touch it, thinking, *Ellie? . . . Ellie?* His hand didn't get to the windshield. A pain tore across his chest. He grabbed himself with both hands. His mouth sprang open and air burst forth. He managed to get his mouth shut before the final invasion of water. The pain, terrible now, curved around his back and into his legs. He began to spin above the seats, pulling at his clothes as if to pull the pain out of himself. Finally he could resist no longer: his mouth opened and the water poured in. The pain shot to all of his extremities. His arms glided to the sides and he floated upward. In the last instant of consciousness there was no pain.

The fish's face was pressed against the windshield, its eyes following the ascent of his body, which had turned and was floating forward. The fish waited, its eyes still now. Soon its body and his body lay head-to-head. The movements of the fish's side-fins imitated the movements of his arms. His body receded toward the back of the car. Watching it, the fish glided forward, bumped the windshield slightly, turned, and swam away.

The Disciple

My mother and my father never kissed and my father was a scrawny man and she was a big woman, big as a mountain, and they never kissed and rarely spoke and I sat between them and listened to their forks click-clacking and waited down the years for them to say something like *Love is just around the corner* or *At the end of every rainbow there lies a pot of gold* or God knows what, waited and waited but nothing was ever said, I give you my word, unless you want to count the fights when he shouted *Fishwoman!* and she screamed *Cur!* and he kicked doors and she threw herself on the sofa and I ran from one prison of a room to another until I found my bed and lay down and swallowed it all through my ears and thought myself a saint.

He was a white old man, round and soft like my mother and there was dandruff on his wild eyebrows and cassock shoulders. I always sat right beside him at the desk in the chaplain's office and sometimes he put his hand on my shoulder as I spoke. His breath smelled like fresh milk boiling.

So you want to be a priest, Michael.
Yes I do, Father, very much.
And why do you, Michael?
To help the world, Father.
That's noble, Michael, that's noble. A Jesuit like me?
No, Father, I'd rather be a parish priest working with families.

It's a fine calling just the same. There's more than one way to serve God.

The student who was closest to friend got a car and we went to the movies together on Friday nights and then he asked two girls from his neighborhood and they came with us and we went to the drive-in and I sat in back and held Marjorie's hand until one night he told us he'd brought something to put in the Cokes. The girls giggled and looked at each other and went to the rest room and came back and said *All right, Arthur, you can put it in.* He got the Cokes and put it in and then even the screen credits became funny and all the cars around us started dancing and Arthur's head got big and then shrunk and I laughed and they looked at me. Marjorie's dress was up and I sent my hand to her thigh and she yelled but I squeezed and didn't let go and Arthur said *Stop!* so I did. Then Marjorie cried and threw up.

And why don't you think you're good enough for the priesthood, Michael?

It's some of the things I've been doing, Father. With, with girls.

Girls? Many girls?

One, Father. And it was only once.

That doesn't seem so bad now, does it?

I, I didn't seem to be thinking, Father. I touched her in, in an impure place.

His arm circled my back and he drew me toward him. *The sins of the flesh are the hardest to resist.*

Yes, Father.

At night, Michael, are you troubled by impure thoughts?

Yes, Father, often.

He lowered his head so that his ear nearly touched my shoulder. *Satan works every minute of the day*, he whispered. *Pray, Michael. Pray before you climb into bed and pray to the Blessed Virgin. She will give you strength. When you lie down think of Mary and her Divine Son, think of the suffering they went through for you and for me, Michael, for mankind. When your thoughts are driven down into darkness, think of them.*

We prayed together and afterward he brought me toward him, held me, terribly tightly, said, *You're a lovely boy, Michael, and you'll make a lovely priest.*

When I left he was weeping. Hunched forward, his face in his hands, weeping.

Angelo was still working when I got to the margarine plant after school. It was his job to open the vats and get them ready for me to clean. Angelo always waited beside the vegetable oil vat and told me about himself. Angelo was married. Angelo didn't have any kids. He had a cord in his penis tied so he wouldn't have kids. He had other women. He stayed in the city after work and drank beer and had other women. He took them to a little hotel room if he had money. He took them down under the freeway when he didn't. He stood them up against a pillar under the freeway and did it. He was about thirty and had slit eyes and when he smiled his mouth didn't open. He was very thin and dark and had almost a woman's face. While he spoke he scraped off hardened pieces of vegetable oil from inside the tank and rubbed them together in his hands.

What do you think of that, eh?

What does your wife say?

Hah! I don't tell her.

Doesn't she mind your drinking?

Hah! I'm the boss.

How old are those ladies?

Some old, some young. I go by looks.

Do you, I mean have a tough time, I mean getting them to, I mean?

Listen. They like it more than men. More! Didn't you know that?

No.

They do. Sometimes I could have three, four women. Women are hungry.

You mean the ones you know.

All women. Show me a woman and I'll show you someone I can screw.

Not all women are that way.

Every woman.

Bull, Angelo. I was thinking of my mother.

He stamped his foot. He hit the side of the tank with the flat of his hand. He shouted: *Every woman!*

Angelo was a liar.

I stood by a woman in a side seat on a streetcar and her knee rubbed mine and I leaned away but her knee followed and I looked down and she was pretty with a hard face and I closed my eyes and stood there wanting and not wanting her and her knee moved up between my legs and I imagined it coming all the way up and touching me, stone against stone, and I couldn't breathe. I ran for the exit and down a strange street. I thought she was thumping after me, so sure I could even hear her breathing. I ran until I found my home and then I looked back. She wasn't there and the moment I knew she wasn't there I knew I wanted her.

Father, how would I know if I didn't have a real vocation?

Ah, Michael, that's a matter between you and God. There's no one can tell you but God.

Through my thoughts?

Oh, deeper than that, Michael. It's in here he tells you. He raised his hand, opening it, and slapped it against his chest. *Through the soul.*

It's something you feel then?

Yes, partly that. He folded his hands over his paunch and leaned back in his chair and slowly raised his head and closed his eyes. *A beautiful feeling.*

Yes, Father.

Very beautiful.

Father?

He opened his eyes and smiled at me down his face. *Yes, Michael?*

I don't think I have that feeling.

He closed his eyes again. His face had a placid look, like the look on the fixed face of someone in a coffin. He seemed, in fact, to be dead, peacefully dead, or at least in a very deep and happy sleep. He was smiling, still smiling, smiling certainly. *You do, though, Michael,* he said. *Your eyes are on God.*

But, Father.

Your eyes are on God and though you be tempted night and day they will remain on him.

Father?

The eyes of a boy driven by sin are dark downcast eyes, crusted with lust, the eyes of an . . . the eyes of an animal. I have seen them, Michael. He leaned forward seeming to descend, and his own eyes, round and slightly protruding, opened very wide now, in a stare, fixed on mine. He seemed suddenly terrified, or a little mad. *The eyes tell everything.*

I waited.

He shook his head and said in a businessman's practical way, *Oh, none of us in the priesthood can deny having had our doubts. None of us. But in the end we submitted to the will of God and allowed it to direct us.*

I'm not sure I know how to do that, Father.

He took my hands in his and looked at them. *Say to Jesus,* he whispered, *my will is thine and thine mine. Say that.*

Now, Father?

Yes, now.

My.

My will is thine.

My, will is thine.

And thine mine.

And thine mine.

He raised my hands and pressed them to his lips. *Michael,* he said hoarsely. *Oh Michael.*

I needed my father then, surely it was then I asked him to come with me to the school football game and then that he said it depended on his arthritis and then that my mother said, *Go with him, can't you?* and then that he took his coffee and went to the darkness of the living room and sat in his big chair by the radio and turned on Bach and tilted his great bald head, gazing down at the base of the curtain as though searching for a lost speck of something, and sat there and sat there until the night came and hammered itself into the roof and never gave me an answer. Then he died.

My mother will probably need me to stay home and work after I graduate, Father, so I don't think I'll be going to the seminary after all.

God will find a way. Speak to him. He will find a way.

I went to church every morning and took communion and asked God to do a lot of things, none of which I remember very well, and then just to do anything, clear the air, whatever he wanted, make me want to or not want to go to the seminary, make me know or not know that my father had loved me, make the sadness go out of my mother's eyes or not go out. It was up to him.

My mother took a job running an elevator in a department store and began to drag herself about the house like someone with a wooden leg. Her skin sagged and lost its color and her eyes went under her eyebrows and she spoke in grunts and said rosaries and dropped dishes and coughed and said, *Michael, what on earth are we going to do?* I fled to school in the morning and to my room at night and said, *I don't know, Mother. I don't know.* She soared to the sofa and wept as though I were my father.

Come on, Angelo said, I got a tiny one just for you.
I've got to get home. My mother isn't well.
She's forty-two but likes young guys.
She looks so bad she might have to go to the hospital.
She's five-by-five but like a jumping bean in bed, I guarantee.
She's dying!
She's jumping!
No!
Yes!

I locked my ears and took my mother for walks in Golden Gate Park on Sundays and we bought stale bread and fed the ducks like she said we used to do when I was little. We found abandoned paths and trudged over them, heads down, wearily searching, as though for precious stones. She always grew tired and had to rest on a rock or stump. I stood by her, silent, and then took her arm and led her home.

Arthur said where have you been keeping yourself and I said around I guess and he said I got another car a convertible and am going with this great blonde from Abraham Lincoln and every weekend we go up to her folks' place on the Indian River it's a ball I'm telling you they don't even ask for I.D.'s in the bars and we use the swimming pool at this big resort and you're invited anytime Mike she said bring your friends.

It sounds great, Arthur.

It really is. I'm not kidding.

I wish I could go but I can't. It's hard to explain.

I pictured Arthur's girl and she was golden born out of the sun and I imagined having her naked on my bed and in the back of Arthur's car and on a beach that was like a great white quilt and she loved me more than Arthur and we never told him. It was more fun that way. Poor Arthur.

It's nice you're going to be a priest, Michael.

I've changed my mind, Mother.

Your father would have been happy.

She talked about Father Devlin up at the parish rectory and how he took his mother for rides on his day off and how the two of them walked arm in arm when they went shopping on Saturdays and how there could be no greater reward for a mother, no matter what the sacrifice, and.

Don't count on it, Mother.

I might buy myself a little car and go see you on visiting Sundays. But.

Pack a picnic lunch and the two of us sit on the lawn beside the chapel and.

No.

You'll write to me, won't you Michael? You'll write every day.

I said, *You have to listen, Father. I can't be a priest. I'm sure now I can't. I don't feel it in me.* I said, *Lately, I've been troubled more than ever by impure thoughts.* I said, *I've been fighting them off sometimes, but they're getting worse and make me think I'll never get rid of them all the way.* I said, *How could I be a priest and hear confessions and stand up in a pulpit and tell people what to do if I was always trying to get rid of desires, terrible desires, Father, and I have them every time I look at a girl on the street.* I said, *Father, please listen to me and try to understand. I admire you so much and all the other priests so much and I wish I was a better person but I can't, Father, I just can't.*

He must have nodded a hundred times as I spoke, rocking back and forth in his chair, his eyes leaping whenever I paused, signaling me to go on, do go on, saying yes yes yes, why haven't you had the courage to tell me this before now.

But when I finished he continued to rock and his eyes continued to leap every few seconds, as though all the time he had been listening to someone else, someone saying things he wanted to hear, another boy, a sacred clean boy of his mind.

Finally all of his motion stopped. He was staring at the framed picture of Jesus across the room. Lost to me.

Father?

He did not reply.

Father?

Nothing.

I rose, backed toward the door, left the office. I don't think he saw me.

I almost said yes to Arthur but couldn't because of the scene I kept picturing, me at a brightly lit cocktail lounge with a loud band at the back and lots of people, all gazing with me at a dark corner where an enormous woman in black was bent over a tiny chair and retching until a stream of something poured whitely from her mouth and filled the air with platinum light.

She went to the doctor and the doctor said the cardiogram showed she had probably had an attack in recent months or maybe years for her blood was not getting to where it ought to at the right speed or rate and if she wanted to live more than a few years she would have to take it very easy, very very easy. No job and only light housework at best.

I went to church and told Jesus I knew he'd done it because I wouldn't be the boy she wanted and said I was sorry but promised to work hard to keep up the house. I looked at his aching face and told him I deserved everything, said if it meant I would have to feed her with a spoon or carry her to bed I would do it. I stared at him for a long time, as though he might reply.

Once I saw the chaplain approaching in the hall and was about to say good morning when his eyes, which had momentarily found mine, reached sideways, found those of another boy, stayed on them until he had taken the boy's sleeve, caught his attention. As I passed them he was saying, *Jerry, Jerry, where have you been? I haven't seen you all week.* He sounded very happy.

Angelo said, *C'mon.*
I said, *No.*
He said, *C'mon.*
I said, *No.*
He said, *C'mon.*
I went.

She smelled like the disinfectant in a men's room and took me to her place in an old hotel and came down on me like a lid and called me *Love* and said *Give give give give give!*

I gave nothing. I grabbed my pants and rattled down the noisy stairs and into the city past ranting cars and tinny bars and alleys that were black and voiceless and stumbled and fell into a filthy gutter and bumped my head and came up choking and saw a million specks, brilliant and flooding my eyes. God had sent the universe off like a rocket.

She was face up on the sofa with one immense leg, bare and blue-streaked, over the side. I sat down beside her and rubbed her back.

It's a hard life, isn't it, Michael?

Yes, Mother, it is.

Fire

His fingers curled tightly over her upper arm. She tried to jerk away but couldn't.

"Donald," she said.

He forced her up, moved her ahead of him past reluctant knees, into the aisle, toward the exit. She stiffened once, as though about to stop, but he tightened his hold and gave her a shove, then kept pushing until they had burst through the exit door and were in the dark alley at the side of the movie house.

"Donald."

They turned the corner, hurried through the fog past a post office, a small grocery store, and ice cream stand, stopping when they reached an old Plymouth parked against the curb.

"Please, Donald."

He released her, put his hand into his jacket pocket and removed a small leather key case, which he flipped open and sent to the keyhole of the door. Quickly he turned the key, removed it, flipped the case closed, and returned it to his pocket. He grabbed the handle and the door opened with a groan.

"Get in," he said.

She took a step back, a slender girl with light blonde hair that clung to her sleek skull, framed her small delicately featured face, and set off her dark brown sweater and light brown skirt, both of which held her tightly.

"No," she said, backing a bit more. "I won't."

Behind her several teenagers at the window of the ice cream stand were looking, about six of them, all boys. She seemed to sense them looking. She turned, glanced at them, then turned back to her companion.

He was crouched a bit, holding the door. The light on the pole that arched out over the sidewalk in front of the ice cream store shone off his dark eyes: glittering pinpoints.

"Get in," he whispered.

She didn't move.

He let go of the door, walked slowly around the car, opened the door on the driver's side, slipped behind the steering wheel, and let the door fall closed with a bang.

She stared at the open car door as the engine started, then rumbled steadily. She bent down and looked into the car.

He didn't speak or move. The tip of his chin was fixed and forward above the wheel.

"It was a stupid thing to do." Her voice was suddenly high-pitched. "A crazy thing. Don't you realize that?"

"Get in."

She didn't move.

Behind her the teenagers, still watching, began to speak in low tones. One of them laughed. She blinked at the sound of the laughter. She bent down further.

"Did you hear me?" She crouched beside the door, gazing at him, waiting. When he didn't answer, she said, "Tell me why."

Very slowly his head turned away from her, toward the empty park across the street. He pressed his foot down, making the engine roar until it coughed; then he raised the foot slightly, until the engine hummed.

"No," she said. "I won't get in." She thrust an open hand toward him. "Give me my purse. Give me some money. I'm not going with you." A narrow purse lay beside him on the seat. When he didn't respond, she leaned into the car and reached for the purse.

He turned quickly, grabbing her wrist.

She wiggled and kicked.

He pulled her into the car.

"Stop it!" she said, "Stop it!"

In a moment the car lurched away from the curb. The door fell closed with a slam. He turned the wheel, and they went into a semicircle. Then the car straightened and shot toward the stoplight across from the post office.

She pulled herself up, shaking her head, shaking the dizziness from it. She held onto the top of the seat, looked back. She saw the teenagers. They were watching the car. They were smiling. They waved their arms. The car shot forward and turned sharply. She fell to the side, then down. As she pulled herself up she could hear the voices of the boys, cheering voices.

The car spun onto a gravel patch in front of an unlit cottage just off the highway. Before it came to a complete stop near the two front steps of the cottage, he snapped on the brake with a fierce jerk. "Let's go," he said, but before she could say or do anything he was out of the car.

Shaking, she got out and looked toward the house, where she saw him crouching at the front door, again working with a key. She turned around, as though looking for something else, but there was only the swooping insolent fog, breaking, vanishing on the gravel just in front of her. She could see nothing beyond the gravel. In the far distance a dog howled. She moved slowly toward the cottage.

He turned on the reading lamp over the beaten overstuffed chair in a corner of the living room. The walls on either side of the chair were yellow and peeling. He turned to her at the door and signaled her to come to the chair.

She went instead to the lumpy sofa next to the front window and slunk down at the end of it, hunching her shoulders, looking fiercely up at him.

"You're stronger than I am," she said. "That's the only reason I'm here."

"Bitch," he said softly, taking a cigarette from his jacket pocket and lighting it.

"The only reason."

"Bitch," he repeated in the same tone. He sat down on the arm of the chair and studied her.

She straightened her stockingless legs and began to tap the toes of her low-heeled shoes together, seeming to smile to herself as she watched the toes touch and move apart, touch and move apart, touch and move apart.

"What was it?" she said. "That his name was Donald?"

"Don't make it small," he said.

She let out a staccato laugh. "That's all I said. I nudged you and said, 'Donald.' That's all."

His lips tightened.

She seemed increasingly amused. "His name was Donald and he was a prissy man, and I turned to you and said 'Donald.' " She laughed. It was a derisive laugh. She looked at him. "You child," she said. "You baby!"

He stood and walked to the window facing the yard at the back. He gazed out, able to see nothing but his own reflection. He stood there for a few minutes. Then he brought his foot back and kicked, sending it into the paperboard wall. He backed away from the window, returned to the chair, sat down on the arm once more, and looked at her blankly.

"It was little," she said, seeming frightened. "Too little a thing for that." She pointed to the black hole in the wall. Then: "What's the matter with you?"

The question floated in the air.

He sat, his eyes fixed on the hardwood floor. At last he said, "We had a fight." He looked up. "When was it?"

Now she was ignoring him.

"Five days ago? A week? Ten days? Then you pouted. Said nothing. Until tonight. Tonight you asked me to take you to the movie. I took you. For what? So you could laugh at me?"

"Fool!"

"You didn't say a word all the way down in the car. All you did was sit in the movie and notice that jerk's name was Donald and then laugh every time his wife snuck away with the . . . the hunter. Why?"

She was looking at her playful toes again, refusing to speak.

"Do you want things to get worse? Is that it?"

She listened, nothing more.

"C'mon," he said. "Is that it? You want to walk out? You want me to? Is that it?"

She looked up at him as though he were a stranger, and her large eyes found and set themselves calmly on his. She gave him no reply.

He remained on the arm of the chair for a while, looking at her. Then he stood and walked past her, walked through the small kitchen at the center of the house, into the single bedroom, where he turned on the light, moved to a bureau and picked up a flashlight which was face down on the top. He switched on the light and went out the door at the corner of the bedroom.

He walked to the foot of the yard. Unkempt grass became visible in the cone of light that moved ahead of him. He stopped and inserted the flashlight into a V formed by two lower branches of a squat oak tree. He adjusted the light so that it shone on a nearby stump. Between the stump and the oak tree was a pile of small logs, about a dozen. The logs seemed to have been resting beside the tree for a long time, for their blackish barks were cracked and withered and the ends of the logs were dark, almost as dark as the barks. He removed one of the logs and placed it on the stump. An old axe lay on the grass, partly hidden beneath the bottom of the pile. He reached down and pulled the handle, causing some of the logs to topple to the grass. He held the axe head up to the light. It was covered with rust. He touched the blunt blade, rubbing his fingers up and down, balancing it in a vertical position. He stepped back, raised the axe and quickly but clumsily brought it down, catching only an edge of the log, sending the log off the side of the stump, almost undamaged. He bent down, picked up the log, and replaced it on the stump. Once more he raised the axe and brought it down, this time more smoothly, more certainly. It entered the top of the log at the center, perfectly straight. He raised the axe again and this time the log rose with it. He brought them both down in a great arc, hitting the stump in the center. There was a loud crack; the log had begun to split. Once more he brought the axe and log up and swung them down. This time the axe went several inches deeper into the log.

Grunting, he repeated his swing a third time. This time the axe moved only an inch or so, then stopped with a clanking sound. He raised the axe and log once more, then brought them fiercely down. Again the clanking sound; the axe would go no further. Tugging, he removed the axe, held it against the light, saw that there was a nick in the blade that hadn't been there before. He dropped the axe and picked up the log, holding the split part to the light, peering into the split. There was a black bar, metal, perhaps iron, about a half-inch in diameter. He pulled frantically, trying to get the two sides apart; they wouldn't move. He turned the log to the left, then to the right. Oddly there were no marks on the bark, no place where the iron bar, or whatever it was, seemed to have entered. He stood puzzling for a few moments, then set the log down on the ground and inserted the axe blade part-way into the split, twisting it, pulling at the butt of the blade; the sides remained where they'd been. He picked up the log and examined it again. There seemed to be no way, with the tools he had, that he could get it apart. He dropped the axe and put the log down, not on the pile from which he'd removed it but a few feet from the pile, as if he might be going to return to it. He walked slowly to the tree, took down the flashlight and started back across the yard.

She was in bed when he entered, flashlight still on. She stirred a bit, then sat up, watching him cross to the bureau, where he turned off the flashlight and set it down.

"What did you prove?" she said.

He didn't reply. He unbuttoned his shirt. Then, before removing it, opened his pants, letting them fall to the floor.

"Donald?"

He turned, toward the inner door, seeming to notice for the first time that the reading lamp in the living room was still on. He made his way through the kitchen and into the living room, and he turned off the lamp. He came back, as sure-footed in the darkness as he had been in the light. He entered the bedroom unpeeling his shirt.

She waited until he was lying beside her then sat up and turned to him. He was on his back on top of the blankets. She bent close, edged toward him, sending her leg lightly against his.

He didn't move.

She waited.

He slid his arm beneath the small of her back and pulled her toward him so that she was lying nearly on top of him, like a blanket.

She sent her hands into his hair, as though trying to uproot it. Gripping the hair, she pulled his face close to hers.

"You'd like to leave me, wouldn't you?" she said.

He turned his head, didn't answer.

"But you're not going to, are you?"

He didn't speak.

"Are you?" she said sharply.

He wouldn't answer.

She sent her knees down over the outsides of his legs, tightened them.

He lay silent beneath her.

Finally he spoke: "Call me someone else's name."

"Whose name?"

"I don't know."

"The hunter's name?" she said with a laugh.

"No!" He struggled a bit, closed his eyes. "An . . . an animal's name."

She moved and the bed began to rock. "You're a forest animal," she said, "a wolf or a fox."

"Yes."

She moved rapidly now.

His eyes were closed.

The bed creaked like trees in a violent wind.

The Pony Track

What I do is draw. Not paint. I draw in black and white. They pay me to stay here because I am getting to be a well-known drawer. Nobody understands what I draw. What difference? It is fashionable these days to have an artist on the staff. So they keep me.

What I do I do. It is all I have left. My wife, what is she? My kid, what is he? Balloons. They are big lead balloons. I look at them and turn away. They are hooked on my belt. I drag them around. My legs go into the ground. Down down down. They are pretty, smiling, right beside me. Down we go.

The man next door is the head of the psychology department where I teach. I don't like him, never speak to him unless I must. But he is sweet on my wife. Gives her a lot of advice about the kid. The kid has a lot of trouble. Nightmares. Elephants come into his room. When the kid started having nightmares the expert told her why. He said the father's an artist, right, and artists are generally introverted, right, and an introverted father might not pay as much attention to his son as others, right? Yes yes yes, she said, delighted at the responsibility getting tossed my way. So, he said, there must be compensations. The kid will do strange things. He cited taking wee wee out of pants when my department chairman was in living room, having tantrums at inconvenient times, and trying frantically to identify me (i.e., elephant). Compensate, give him what he wants. He'll have a harder time finding his own way than a kid with a normal father. Such was the expert's message.

I thought of suing. First him, then my wife who believed him like a god. I thundered through the house when she told me. I kicked over the coffee table and broke a lamp. I went upstairs and woke up the kid and shook him. But then, shaking the kid, I knew I wouldn't sue anyone. I let go of him and he fell back on the bed, thinking, I guess, that it was only another nightmare. I went weakly downstairs.

Sue who? Sue Freud? Jung? Adler? Horney? Sullivan? Fromm? Spock? I must have been crazy. They had the books, the knowledge, the law. What had I? My madness, that thing all the critics see in my drawings. She threatened to call the police, my neighbor, have me committed. I knew she would. I pleaded, don't, it's over. I pleaded for a couple of hours. All right, she said, as long as we raise the kid her way. Yes yes yes, I said, terrified, not meaning it.

Take him to the circus, she said. It's the least you can do. Show him a real elephant. Maybe his nightmares will go away. Hold his hand. Be his friend. Try.

I didn't want to take him. I don't like taking him anywhere. I said, if he stops seeing elephants he'll see something else—flies, dogs, frogs. What's the use of taking him?

Go, she said, take him. I'm sick of you being around the house on Saturdays.

I take the kid. I am curious about what I'm going to be after he sees a real elephant. But he does what he would have to do, being him. He tells me to buy popcorn and a cone of spun sugar. It's his day. I buy. He doesn't eat. I think he will eat when we get into the big tent. I show him the pretty wagons, I show him the barker, I show him the pony rides. Want a pony ride, I say. He takes my hand and leads me to the pony track. The popcorn is spilling. The cone is melting. He has the popcorn under his arm and the cone in his hand. They are both about to drop as he pulls me along. I say, let me help. I reach down to take one or both, to help him. He screams, shouts no, jerks his hand from mine, darts under the pony track fence, nearly getting kicked in the head by a passing pony. He carries his cone and popcorn to the grassy circle in the middle of the track. He plops down. He starts pouring the popcorn into the spun sugar. He looks up smiling at all the kids going by him on their ponies. The kids start pointing to him. Some parents laugh. The ticket taker shakes his head. Now I see him eating the popcorn out of the cone. Each kernel has a coat of pink spun sugar. He is an ugly kid to begin with. Now the popcorn, some of it, sticks to his cheeks and chin, and he is even uglier. Hey, stupid, look what you're doing, says an older kid on a pony. But other kids and the parents are roaring. What a show. Only the ticket taker seems nervous, the ticket taker and me. I am backing away, toward the parking lot, in my heart disowning the kid, never wanting to see him again, being a hater of crowds to begin with, a hater of attention, a hater of precocious kids especially. Running backwards. A crowd gathers. Watching a popcorn-and-spun-sugar beard grow on a little kid at the center of a pony track. Who the hell does he belong to, shouts the ticket taker as his eyes leap from the ponies, which are bunching up restlessly, to the crowd, which is getting larger and larger. I go faster, faster. Who, he demands. I am in the parking lot, still going. I slam into the grill of a car and its horn blows. In the car someone is cursing at me. I don't even look. I dive to the ground and crawl around the car, stopping only to glance back and see that the pony track is surrounded with people, people who are rushing out of the main tent and the side show tent and winding around the pony track, pointing and laughing. The last thing I see is the ticket taker leaping over the inner fence, going after him. Capture him, I scream silently to the ticket taker and I turn and go like a snake past Buicks and Fords and Chevrolets and Pontiacs and Mercurys and trucks and tractors and wagons and bikes and cycles and gas stations and drive-ins and houses. Oh, I want to lie down and sleep. But I don't. I stumble, scramble, leap and dive, for miles. After I pull myself up the front steps I see my wife at the door. In her arms is the kid. He fainted, she said. He fainted and they took him home. Where were you?

All afternoon and evening I drew. Wild pictures, a million lines in each, or rather one line in each that turned and twisted about itself until something emerged—the face of an old man in one, a fierce hatchetlike instrument in another, even an elephant. When I see something emerge, a suggestion, I stop. That's my way. Food for fame. I stuffed them in my desk drawer and went home. The incident at the circus? What incident? Drawing does great things. I'd forgot.

But I went home and into the living room and there the neighbor is sitting with my kid on his lap and my wife too cozily close to him. What's this?

I'm leaving you, she says.

I pick up the glued-together lamp and threaten.

That won't solve anything, says the expert.

The kid is calm, happy looking.

I hold the lamp poised in the air. Tell me. I hear my voice quivering. Anger is shattering into fear. Say it. Tell! Why, why, why!

Maxwell thinks it best, she says.

Maxwell is the expert. He is watching, studying me. He is slick, neat, gray-haired, masterful, and very calm. My kid eases close to him.

Despite the shock I still have some strength. Get out, I utter.

I'm afraid she's right, he says, deaf to me, it's best for all concerned.

Get out or I'll kill you, I whisper.

He stands calmly, lifts the kid, my kid, and carries him past me, beneath the lamp, to the stairs. To bed now, he says, like some father on television, and the kid scampers, hops, flits up the stairs, his every footstep bespeaking an effort to please. The expert returns to the sofa, sits down, takes my wife's hand.

I stare.

Angela, he goes on, wishes me to stay with her tonight in case you decide to come back during the late hours. She's, frankly, frightened.

It's unfortunate, he says with a frown, that the stewardship of the home and creative artistry are so often incompatible.

I live here, I shout, and I release the lamp but miss him by from seven to ten feet and he darts forward, gets me in a professional neck lock, sends me to the floor, and instructs Angela to call the police, which she does.

My being committed has enhanced my position as an artist. They seem now to really think I'm a genius. I have heard that the two galleries who show and market my work in the city are getting twice what I got before I was locked up. The director of one of the galleries wrote me recently and made what I suppose he thought was a good joke: We are planning to distribute little biographies of you to people who come in. Could you give us some vivid details of your hallucinatory experiences so that we might add them to the biography? People are very interested in you personally.

My doctor is an old and curious man who finds it interesting and significant that I draw in black ink only and have no desire to use colors. I asked him why. He smiled patiently and said I would have to tell him and not he me. I have never thought about why I use black-and-white as opposed to color. I have no idea. My being released, however, seems to depend somewhat on my discovering why. I suppose I will have to try. I told the doctor that I would learn why after I had consulted my liver. He turned over a page of the writing pad on his desk, picked up his pencil, looked at me and said, your liver? Go on. I didn't go on. His questions took all the fun out of going on.

Angela wrote and said that when the doctor feels it's safe she's going to bring the kid for a visit. He may as well learn to face reality at an early age, she said. That sounded to me like one of the expert's perversions. And it probably was. He spends, according to Angela, many afternoons at our house consulting with her. He has no children of his own and last Saturday he took the kid to the last performance of the circus. The kid, she wrote, was perfectly behaved and enjoyed the elephants most of all. The expert lives with his crippled mother, being as yet unmarried. Angela said in conclusion that the mother adores the kid and wants him over at the house virtually every moment. It gives her, Angela, a lot of free time. For consultation no doubt.

My department chairman wrote me and said the college would have to remove me from the regular staff. They will, instead, make me a part-time lecturer, he said. I trust you understand, he concluded. I don't.

I haven't drawn for days until this morning. I drew one thing, a line, diagonally across a page of white paper. Very pretty. I folded the paper at the line. I tore it at several evenly spaced places along the edges. I put a pin in the middle of the page, of the line, and bent every other torn section, making little flaps like wings. I opened my window and reached through the bars, releasing the paper. It spun slowly downward, away from the building. It landed on a duck pond. It became wet and clung to the water. It floated beneath some reeds. Part of it went under. Part of it, a little tip, sticks out, pointing upward, toward me and the building. Water laps over the tip now and then but so far it always pops back up. One of these times it won't pop up. I stand at the window waiting for it not to pop up.

Cold Places

That morning he was at the front of the sofa looking under with his padded bottom toward me and I saw a button open at the side of his snow pants and thought of closing it and he said *find my mitten, Dad,* and I said *find it yourself* and forgot to close the button.

In the photograph. He is at the center. Marked by the brightest light. He is my son, just three. He is laughing at the speechless infant beside him, his sister. He is my son and his soft hair is growing outward, toward the door and the curtain and the camera, growing growing everywhere.

To his left, holding the baby, his mother. She is smiling vaguely toward the kitchen and wondering if the candles have burned down into the chocolate. She has not been out of this house in six days because there is a baby and the weather has been cold. She has sat in the mornings at the window in an antique rocking chair we got at an auction and painted white, and every morning she has held the baby's mouth concealed to her nipple and watched her boy, three, in the catalpa tree.

One day she said *guns, nothing but guns.*
I said *I'd like him to stop.*
She said *it must be the age.*
I said *it doesn't matter what it is.*
She said *what can we do if the others play with them.*
I said *he has a mind, is old enough to see killing on the screen, old*

enough to believe guns solve something, therefore old enough to learn they can't.

What can he know of death at his age?

Death comes to all ages.

It's part of growing up, those guns. Let him play.

I was going to speak to him but I forgot until he crept between my legs one evening and held the neighbor boy's plastic .45 to my face and said *fum, fum, fum. Got you, Dad. Fall down.* I stepped back to get position to bend after him but caught my foot on his tractor and stumbled as though I might be playing and he laughed, oh how he laughed, his hands like jelly wiggling in the air just above the floor, one of them with the quivering pistol. I grabbed the gun. I threw it toward the front door. I said *up to bed.* I chased him to the bottom of the stairs. *Up*! I shouted. Up he went.

He said later *it was just pretend.*

I shook my head.

She nudged me as though I hadn't heard.

He can try something else, I said. *There must be something else.*

He won't like it.

I'll talk to him. I'll see what else there is. He'll tell me.

But he didn't.

He talked only about guns.

What did they do with guns? They went into the bushes on the other side of the fence near the doctor's house. Into the tall trees the three of them went and killed a tiger. He used to tell me about it at night. He said *we killed a tiger.* To him a fact. *A very big tiger. He had hair on his teeth. And wanted to take us away. And eat our legs. He came into my room last night. I killed him. If he comes tonight I kill him again.* He killed the tiger a lot. *The* tiger, always the same. Death was not death.

I stopped him. He watched from this side of the fence while the other two hunted. She said it was sad to see him watching from this side.

Once, she said, while the other two were hunting, he went up the catalpa, a broad tree with thick branches, nearly perfect for climbing. He went all the way up and then out on one of the branches to watch the others or maybe spy a tiger. She signaled him from the window: be careful. He smiled back at her now as he is smiling up at me now. *Bravely*, she said.

It was my birthday. I gave him a gift. It was late but he wanted to hunt again. Maybe I was impressed with the way he'd wrapped my present in a newspaper. Maybe I was delighted to hear he had put powdered soap on the cake, thinking it was frosting. Maybe he lisped just right when he said *Happy Birthday*. I don't know. *Yes yes*, I said, *go hunt*. It was after supper. We took a picture. He still couldn't find his mitten. The baby fell asleep. He went out with one hand in his pocket. She and I had *creme de cacao* in tiny glasses. It was the quietest hour of the day.

The neighbor man ran in with him and placed him on the sofa and someone had gotten the doctor and the doctor came quickly and took out a knife and opened his throat. I held her and the doctor worked over him and then looked up at us and shook his head and said *it doesn't help* and she said *No*! She fell forward and I held her and she twisted her head and screamed up the curtains into the universe, "TIGERS!" then went limp and sank from my arms. The doctor drew back. *He was choking*, he said. *The strap from the gun got caught on the fence. It must have been only seconds*. I rushed forward and I smothered my son with the bulk of me but he was dead.

We took a photograph and he couldn't find his mitten and the cake tasted funny and the other two had already gone over the fence and he followed but the strap hooked on the top and he fell and the strap twisted and his feet didn't touch the ground.

She is gone.

And the baby, the baby is gone too.

My sister came, and her husband.

The man on the radio kept saying six above zero.

Someone else came.

Bill. My friend Bill came. The photograph had come out of the camera alive and I was holding it when Bill came. I said *look*. *Look at him growing!*

Stop it!

He's only three!

Ben!

I could feel myself trembling apart. I could feel myself trembling and my body must have been smarter than my mind, for it held, waiting for Bill, and now Bill was here and I was going, could feel myself going down.

Ben!

Down and into little pieces which would enter the floor and go into the earth where I'd find and become my boy.

Ben!

I knew how impossible my notion was even as I was falling but I could not stay up. I fell forward and hit my face. The pain turned to numbness and reached out. I felt his hands. *Get up*, he said.

I got up.

He said *sit there and don't move*. He said *I'll get you a drink.*

I shouted, *I had a drink. Then he died.*

He held me.

I said *his throat spoke blood! Ugh! Look at it on the cushion beside you! He's dead!* I screamed it.

Bill wouldn't look at me.

I wept.

When I stopped he said *he* is *dead. Face it!*

We teach literature, Bill and I. I watched him. He was weeping. Literature says in death there is rebirth. Literature is full of hope. Literature is rebirth. Something lives on. Nothing lives on. It is a lie, an illusion. One survives or doesn't. If that's living on, something lives on. I was thinking. I was on the sofa thinking and looking at Bill on the floor who was weeping. Did he believe in what we teach? In rebirth, literature, Western Civilization? The recurrence of the day? Sperm? *Well?* I shouted it: *Well?* Then I tore the photograph into small pieces and it fell from my hands, the pieces.

I say to myself over and over night and day do what you want and say what you want because the creators we have created provide us with necessary myths that need not be clothed in drawings or speeches or print but are somehow part of us invisibly transmitted through flesh of all flesh from instant first. I don't believe any of that. But I must attest.

I do.

I attest to that string-haired creature at the Ogdensburg hospital, to her rocking with an armful of air on a dirty floor in the sight of stone-faced nurses or to her doctor's saying I think it may be months and not weeks. I attest to my cursing my sister who came for the baby and to my sending Bill away and to my running out into the street later a spectacle to the neighbors wailing like a child abandoned. I attest to going alone to the catalpa late at night and hugging its thick trunk and speaking *Ben Ben Ben*. I attest to the ice on the front porch I can't peel away and to the light in the living room I won't turn off and to the snows that follow the snows that have come down here in the days since he died.

I attest to all that will happen or will not and the possibility that there will be another son or that there will not be another son and that he will climb the catalpa or not climb the catalpa and play with guns or not play with guns and die before me or not before me. I attest even to the denial of these possibilities because in my denial there is strength I don't understand but trust as I do the inevitability of the night.

I have cursed up the spine of God and down the galaxies of the universe. I have shucked idea and gesture. I have violated love. I have stood alone, my only god. In some kind of defense against annihilation I took to myself a woman and she bore me a child and a child and I led them all with certitude which was pride and they vanished now I am alone. Now. I. Am. Alone. In each there is a possibility. Choice has been shaved to the skin.

On our corner there lives a very old man. Each night I bring hamburger or stew and cook it in his apartment. We eat silently. He lights a very black pipe and walks to his tiny window. If there is snow he says *snow*. If there are no stars he says *dark*. If there are voices he says *people*. He has two rooms. He walks from the kitchen to the one in front where he sleeps and sits. He draws the curtains. I bring him coffee. He puts it on the little table beside his ancient chair. He waits. Finally he raises his fist and then, once, hammers just below his chest, then again. I wait. There is a long low rumbling burp, as certain as the night. It is followed by a wheeze of relief. *Late*, he says as he picks up his coffee. Yes, late. Later every night. Yes. The light on the wall has fallen down. He looks at the closed curtains. *Late*, he says. I nod. He falls asleep in the chair. I have offered to help him to bed. He always shakes his head. He will go to bed in his own time. And he does.

I walk home slowly. My feet are heavy in the snow.

The house is always empty, always cold.

I lie down next to the sofa every night and every night I reach down and touch, squeeze, the mitten that is there. I hold it and I do not weep but remember Ben's smile, not the one in the photograph, *his*. It is the most possible. I press the mitten to my face, speak his name and then lay it back where it was. The house is cold, very very cold.

The Chairman's Party

At the end of the first week there was a party at the chairman's house. The house was old, wooden Victorian, and had a tower on the left, near the front door. After she opened the door for us, the chairman's wife said, "Welcome to Tara, as done by Charles Addams." Then she laughed. Marcy smiled at her and we went in.

I had had diarrhea all afternoon. It was still with me when we got to the party.

The chairman's wife took our coats and led us to the punch bowl. She introduced us to someone and then to someone else. The punch was turbid and dullish yellow. The chairman's wife said, "We love weird houses and always have. That's why we bought this one. Everything creaks. You're never alone." She smiled at Marcy.

I went to the bathroom. It was at the base of the tower, near the living room. Most of the people were in the living room, sitting in chairs forming a rectangle. When I came out of the bathroom, I found a stray chair, outside the rectangle, just a few feet from the bathroom door.

At the center of the rectangle, on a wooden base, stood a car's tailpipe and muffler, bronzed. The tailpipe seemed to grow out of the wooden base. It twisted and turned, moving upward, and at the top was the muffler, off at a slight angle. People looked at it when they talked, even when they weren't talking about it. I heard the chairman's wife tell someone that their house guest, a Mr. Prato, had purchased it from one of the college's art students for seventy-five dollars earlier in the week. Mr. Prato, she said, had insisted on having it put at the center of the living room for the party. "So the conversation won't die." She laughed. Her laugh was like the pained cry of a small girl whose mouth is being held. The laugh did not go with her face, the face that had appeared at the front door, the face that had since passed before me several times.

I went to the bathroom a second time but could expel only gas. I opened the window and looked out to the front lawn with its tufts of snow and then to the street with its cars hunched like rhinos crouching. I let the antiseptic wind blow in. A stray stiff elm leaf blew down, landing on the sidewalk. A tan dog passed across the lawn and disappeared at the side of the house. A car's headlight flashed along the sides of the parked cars but no car moved down the street. When I felt sure the last residue of odor had vanished I closed the window. I listened to the wind hissing at the sills and to the sounds, garbled, from the living room. I returned to my chair.

Someone said, "One daughter, she's studying at Rochester or Syracuse. Music, I think."

"I'd like to meet her."

"She doesn't come home often." The speaker, a woman, lowered her voice. "She's going with a Negro boy. It's caused some trouble." She was whispering but her voice seemed to carry better than when she had been speaking in normal tones. "So I've heard at least. They don't talk about it."

"Those things aren't uncommon anymore."

"Still . . ."

They were interrupted. The chairman had led Mr. Prato to their place and was introducing him. I heard "Marvelous," and, "No, but Charles's aunt vacations there every year," and "You look a little like that actor, Sir Cedric Hardwicke. Has anyone told you?" Mr. Prato made grunting noises.

The chairman left Mr. Prato with the two women and came over to my chair.

"What do you think of our friend's masterpiece?" he said, pointing to the sculpture.

I told him I had never seen a tailpipe shaped quite like that. I told him I thought it was interesting, not only the sculpture itself but the fact that it had been placed at the center of the living room. I told him I thought of oil and dirt when I thought of tailpipes and mufflers and such, but I did not think of them when I looked at this muffler and tailpipe.

His mouth seemed to widen a little with each of my statements. When I finished he was nodding. "That's the whole point, isn't it? I mean about this modern stuff. What they *do* with what's around us. Not the stuff itself but what they *do* with it."

Mr. Prato had moved to another side of the rectangle.

After saying, "At first I wasn't sure, but now I like it, like the idea of it, like the way it puts things in a new light," the chairman followed him.

Earlier Marcy had asked me if I wanted to go to the party. I said no.

She said, "It's the first. Once the introductions are over, we won't be required to go to others."

"You can call and tell them I'm sick. I am."

"It's the oldest excuse in the world. They won't believe me."

"Then tell them a lie, even though that's the truth."

"This one we have to go to. Put up with it, for an hour or so."

I watched her across the room now, head tilted, nodding as she looked at the sculpture and listened to the woman beside her who was speaking rapidly.

I felt several sharp pains in my abdomen and went to the bathroom but couldn't release anything.

Several people came separately and sat in the empty chair near mine and chatted with me. One spoke about the sculpture and one about the way the college was growing and one about the things there were to do in this part of the country. She mentioned auctions. "I don't know what I'd do without the auctions," she said. "You can pick up antiques—absolutely authentic antiques!—for prices that are dirt cheap."

"Nothing is certain," said the woman who had told the other about the daughter. "That's why I won't comment. They see things differently now. Who are we to say?"

"I only mean what it does to the parents. We have rights too."

"I couldn't bear it. But I don't know what I'd do. That's why I won't comment."

"You're a noble woman, Melody. I mean it. I wouldn't put up with it. I just wouldn't."

"I'm not saying that I would, or could, but . . ."

I had gone upstairs after agreeing to attend the party. Marcy was on the bed, resting for the party. Darkness had descended into the room, blunting all the objects. In the dull light her slip, all she was wearing, faintly shimmered, billowing out over her buttocks. I sat down beside her and sent my hand lightly up one of her legs. I touched the soft hair and the warm crease between.

"There isn't time."

The babysitter had arrived, was downstairs in the kitchen with Bumbo.

Still I extended my forefinger, moved it gently about, against the sliding nugget beneath.

"It isn't fair. There isn't time."

Recently I had seen a girl with long brown legs sitting on a porch step with two companions. One leg was extended over several stairs but the other was up, foot resting on the step beneath the one on which she was sitting. I was crossing the street toward them and could see the strip of black panties over her crotch. I glanced up to see that the girl with the long brown legs and her two companions, less attractive girls, were watching me. But the legs widened a bit. I stared into them and approached, as if I were going to go through the girls and up the stairs. The legs did not close. When I reached the sidewalk before them, the three girls were smiling at me. I hesitated, smiled back, then turned and started home.

Now looking at Marcy on the bed, I wanted to tell her about the girl with brown legs. "Does it bother you?" I would have said.

"When we come back," she said.

"No, now. We haven't done anything in days."

Whether it had bothered her or not, I would have pretended she was the girl with the brown legs. Perhaps, beginning now, I would pretend each time that she was a different person. Eventually I would tell her. She, too, might begin to pretend. We would disguise ourselves to each other. If she didn't want to disguise herself, there might arise a new tension between us, something to occupy us, something to work at erasing.

She had twisted up, was sitting on the side of the bed, looking lovely.

I reached out to touch her but she stood.

"When we come back," she said.

Mr. Prato was standing near the tailpipe and muffler and seemed to be lecturing about it.

The door opened for someone leaving and the cold wind splashed against the side of my face.

Marcy looked at me from across the room, glanced at the door, then back at me. I nodded.

I got our coats.

At the front door the chairman said I had put it as well as anyone, about the sculpture. "I'll bet," he said, "those sophomore humanities classes of yours will be . . . compelling." His wife stood behind him, smiling at both of us.

In the car Marcy said the woman who had been sitting beside her told her the chairman's wife was going to have to have one of her breasts removed in a few days. "They haven't told the daughter," she said. "She doesn't know how serious it is."

The streets were slippery. At one corner, trying to stop, I made the car skid into a cross street. Had a car been coming along the cross street it might have struck us. Then I couldn't get the car into the driveway beside our duplex because of a patch of ice. Marcy got out. The car kept slipping back. I finally parked next to the curb.

Marcy had paid the babysitter and was getting into bed when I came in. "They think it's probably too late," she said.

I went into the bathroom. I got down on the floor and bent myself up, abdomen against upper legs, elbows beside knees. I tried to force the pain out of me. There was a prolonged hiss, as if someone behind me were commenting on my efforts. The pain remained, however. I lowered my head to the floor. No relief. Finally, too tired to move, I slept.

Other Lives

I creep out into the cumulus morning, where, slipping from tree to tree down sun-scrubbed streets, I find myself in a communal place, one of the last retreats of the lately civilized.

Above and somewhat before me stand a man in white frock with the sort of facial declivity I have never, for more than a few minutes running, been able to bear without repulsion going to nausea—broad unoccupied brow descending past pinhole eyes through sliver of mouth to effective chinlessness.

"Howdy do," says he.

I nod.

During childhood and adolescence I feared that that face or something like it would claim the forefront of my own cranium, and like a tatoo-nude on the bicep of a hefty sailer, twist obscenely through my later years, mocking me into senility, finally collapsing to a formless flap, difficult guesswork for even the hippest mortician.

A groan.

I turn.

The barber's loud greeting, spoon rattling in a plastic tumbler, has stirred from his nap the old man sitting in the chair by the window; his eyes rise under a gray frown that startles the air between barber and me and suggests, to me at least, that he's been wrenched from a rich and sensual dream whose movements will not be recaptured. The eyes slide wearily toward mine, hold mine for a moment, close slowly, open even more slowly, then return, searching the air, as if he may after all catch a glimpse of the dream's last sweet movements. Finally the eyes go softly closed and the head veers to the left, hangs over the shoulder as if being held by an invisible string.

The barber has moved and now I see in the mirror the face of a young man. It's a face I have encountered at least ten thousand times—full and symmetrical, high cheeked, immaculate, with clear untroubled blue eyes—a face to command the attention of all waking and proximate eyes, an attractive face, a near-perfect face. Another observer, fresh out of the country or touching down from a far planet, given the comparisons available in this room, might very well find it so above reach, beyond assault, that he, she or it would rise in raving applause; I, however, have seen it so often illuminated in magazines, magnified on billboards, blown to outrageous proportions in films, that it has become to me as monotonous as peanut butter or the Pledge of Allegiance.

There is a low growl in the belly of the old man.

The young man smiles at me through the mirror.

I smile back abruptly—there/gone.

I was going to look like the young man when I wasn't going to look like the barber. And there were others, on streetcars, on buses, in parks, heads and faces picked up the way children gather acorns, all borne heavily through the years, each a part of that enormous question about my looks, about more than my looks, about the self behind the looks, that question which remains and may always remain. I have tried to justify it: *because it's a young question, it will keep me young*. I don't know. It's as vital to me as someone else's question about sports, or another's about slim legs. Maybe it's a question I must never answer.

The barber is pointing his clipper at the old man. "He's next."

It's such an obvious remark that I concentrate not on it but on the arcing movements, simultaneous, of the clipper returning from the old man and the barber's eyes returning from me: glidings inward along the wings of a seagull. Eyes and clipper alight together on a lock of hair just above the young man's ear. The barber speaks to me again, this time through the young man's ear:

"If he stays asleep, you can go ahead."

I don't care to go ahead. The old man has his rights. I shake my head.

The barber, concentrating on an angle, doesn't notice.

I'll point my finger at him and say, "Let it remain the way it was. He's first. He goes first."

No.

I'll do it lightly, cross my legs, say with a smile, "Look. This is my day off. I can wait."

No.

I'll look from behind a threatening finger and say, "I'm not getting out of this chair until you cut the hair of that man by the window, even if I have to sit here all night."

There was a flowing gentle order to the way it was going. Why did he have to speak?

Conversation. He wants conversation. Yes. The pleasure of sculpting the blond will soon end and there will have to be something else. He will get no pleasure out of cutting my hair; it is soft and shapeless, simple to cut. The old man will only fall asleep in the barber chair. It is me, my conversation, that interests him. I will give him nothing, now or later. When he signals me to go next, I'll reply with a flick of the hand: *him, not me.*

The young man is again smiling at me through the mirror.

Why?

This time I don't smile back.

Still smiling.

I close my eyes.

Last night, as I passed through the shadows of an elm near a street light, a man, head down, hurried by. Then, from behind us, came the hollow angry voice of a woman: "It was no good! I didn't enjoy it! I never enjoy it!" The man began running and was soon out of reach of the woman's voice: "You have nothing to give me and never will! You fart! You ugly fart!" The man had disappeared and I took the woman's words to myself, for, suddenly, they seemed intended for me: "Look at yourself, you pervert! Look at yourself!"

Later I stood before the full-length mirror behind my closet, saw something menacing in the eyes, thought of a word: *Heinous.* I recalled a newspaper story from years earlier: an old man had been arrested in New Jersey for the rape of a three-year-old girl. "I'm a heinous man and I've lived a heinous life," he told the reporter.

I did not rape a little girl. I did not offend the angry woman.

Who did?

The barber did.

The old man did.

The young man did.

Yes.

The old man lived in New Jersey and raped the little girl, who is now the wife of the barber and the lover of the young man. The old man, then sixty-three, now eighty, was released for senility after sixteen years and followed his sin to this town. He leaves mysterious gifts at the back door of the barber. The barber's wife mistakes them as gifts from the grocer's delivery boy. Consequently, she has invited the delivery boy in for coffee and, after small talk, has confessed her disappointment in her husband, twenty-three years her senior. The delivery boy has recently been shucked by his girlfriend, now a sophomore at a distant college. Her letter, on lightly perfumed buff-colored stationery, said, "You just *haven't* had the kind of experience I need. I'm sorry." The barber's wife has therefore been a godsend to him, and they quickly become lovers. Last night, needing a reason to quiet her conscience, the barber's wife had brandy and made a vague connection: "You're no better than that bastard who raped me! You're two of a kind! Making love to you is no better!" She then kicked the barber out of the house and whipped after him with the words that fell on me. While all of us who sit here are players in the drama, I am the only one aware of the intricacies of our relationship.

I should now stand and say, "I have information to give all of you."

I won't, saving myself, above all, from a conversation with the barber.

I invent my own life and the lives around me. A young woman. Yesterday she had brown eyes and an itch to wander in the woods. Today the eyes darkened and she wished only to sit at the back table in the reading room of the library. These, though I have always seen her standing in the same place at the same time and have detected no real evidence beyond the moods of her eyes: they *seem* this way or that. I've come upon her again and again. Yesterday her eyes, hazel, asked me a question. *Search the books or the woods*, I answered. Then: *I wish you'd say something first.* She didn't. Tomorrow it will be different. In the same place. At the same hour. The same girl.

There is a hiss from the old man.

I look up, say to the barber just above a whisper, "I want *him* to go first." I point to the old man, still asleep.

The barber's scissors freeze above the head of the young man. He glances across at the old man, then at me, lowers the scissors, shrugs. It's a priceless articulate shrug, which says: "You try to do someone a favor and he gives you a lot of shit. All right. The son-of-a-bitch is asking for it. I'll put the old man ahead of him and cut his hair like I'm paralyzed."

Fine. I'm in no hurry.

A groan from the old man.

Not a rapist at all, he is nevertheless dreaming about a rapist, the night-rapist who came in upon his sister, the same whom he, then young, discovered and bludgeoned, savoring the tiger cub's first taste of blood. He carried it down the years, like a soldier his memory of first battle, longed to meet the rapist again, searched for real approximations, in barroom battles, factory tangles, his bullyings of his wife, but never found anything to match that first full feast. He swelled in anger at the injustices of such a life. Later he learned that the rapist hadn't even laid a hand on his sister, that she had been coquettish, that in fact there had been earlier meetings between the victim and his sister, that there was indeed the suggestion of an invitation. For these he forgave her, forgave all but the circumstances that had crippled his hopes for a violent odyssey. Would he never surprise another intruder? A hold-up man? More than once he has daydreamed of driving his automobile swiftly over a small child.

"Look at the records."

"Mmm."

The contradiction before me now sustains itself, for the moment at least, in an exchange of trivia that an entering dunce might credit as conversation. The barber, realizing he can expect nothing but silence from me, has peeled the hide off a subject as suitable as any for a citizen of this Republic. I don't think he really cares any more than the young man—nodding now, nodding—that the Giants are the ones to bet on because they have the highest fielding average in the league and no one counts fielding anymore but look at the fielding averages of all the pennant winners over the past twenty-five years. It's an opening, that's all, and if he's lucky the young man's nods will turn to speech, maybe argument. There is harsh music in the barber's seesawing metaphors, uncommon blasphemics and miscellaneous grunts; and, with a few more "yes, but's" and "I like's" from the young man, his words could elasticize into a speech with, at least, grammatical integrity. But the young man's nods and phrases are empty promises, and the conversation soon dies, a ball rolling on wet grass.

A silence stirs the air.

The barber gives me a nervous look.

I have nothing to say.

I look at the old man.

So does the barber.

Still asleep.

Were I too to sleep, would I, could I, meet him in his dreams, or mine? More than the mystery of facade is the mystery of possibility. The God of the priest is the grave. Doctors long to injure. Criminals are the policeman's heroes. It is not simply: *Nothing appears as it really is.* Or: *Nothing is what it appears to be.* Or even: *All things are the opposite of what they appear to be.* It is . . .

What?

This silence.

Something has stopped.

I *want* to go next.

In nomine patris, et filii, et spiritus sancti.

A flight of swallows has risen out of the linoleum.

No. It's the action of the wind against the door.

The young man, risen from his chair, is still smiling, smiling as he scrapes his pocket for a tip, smiling as he turns to the cash register and scoops his wallet out of back pocket, smiling as he pays the barber.

I'm wrong.

Not smiling.

It's his face. The configurations of his face, his expression, make it appear that he's smiling, has been smiling. He was born to that expression or trained to it. Not a smile. He may be frightened, sullen, angry. His look, nothing more. Nothing may have broken through to him here, from the barber, me, the old man. He may be blind and stone-deaf.

Going out now.

That look like a smile is still there.

I don't know anything about him.

Or about the barber.

Or about the old man.

We are separated from each other by eons.

The barber is standing beside the old man, looking across at me: "Well?"

"Him," I say quickly.

He must understand, not ignore me, not come forward, beckon me to the barber chair. I *don't* want to go first now. I *don't* want to stay here. When the old man is in the barber chair, I'll leave. It is important that he take the old man.

He bends down and nudges the old man.

The elbow slides off the silver arm of the chair, head snapping down, torso bending. It's a contortion that would be difficult even for a supple child. He makes no sound.

"Hey." The barber touches his shoulder.

The old man just hangs there, motionless.

The barber's eyes climb to mine.

I know what's happened. I watch the barber's bloodless lips twist open, and I expect the low humor of a back-street comic: *I guess you're next, after all. Har! Har!* I actually plan to force a laugh when I hear it. I'm grateful to the barber and all the forces that control him when I don't. He merely whispers, "Jesus Christ."

We stand before each other, the barber and I. He knows what comes next or it will invent him. He is trying to speak. I am trying to speak. Our eyes are locked. I see my fright in his. Words won't come. His head is moving slowly from side to side. Is mine?

He waits.

I reach out, take hold of his thin forearm. I want to speak but I can't. Instead I release his arm, turn, take a couple of steps, reach down, grab the door handle, turn it, yank open the door and flee.

Outside, the street is full of sounds.

I do not see a face I pass.

In the air there is a pungency of rotted leaves.

Getting up the Stairs

I am at the bottom.

There are eleven and not, say, twelve, unless I count the landing at the top, not in fact a stair but a floor, except where it juts out, offering the illusion of stair. To count the landing as a stair, however, opens the possibility of counting the floor I am standing on as a stair, at least that part of it that serves as a stepping-up place. It would be easy for me to add in landing and floor were it not for a problem that has more to do with my own condition than that of the stairway.

I am, I'm afraid, the unliberated son of a religious zealot who crossed herself at the first rumble of distant thunder, said the hand of God was on the steering wheel every time she read about an automobile accident, and cried out to Archangel Michael whenever her liver acted up. Under such circumstances, I would like to calculate a settlement between dreaded thirteen and unattractive eleven—two skinny imponderable *ones*—and give myself and the stairway the attractive number in between, with all its chummy associations: apostles, eggs, months of the year, and such. But of course I can't. To accept the landing as a stair is to accept the floor, and vice versa; to reject one is to reject the other. Fear in me has always overcome uncertainty, and just about everything else.

Eleven, therefore, is my number.

There are other problems.

I weigh approximately 425 pounds and my girth is eighty inches at the most ample part. On that last I must make qualification, for the last time I was measured, by a salesman named Joseph at The Fat Boy's Shoppe, the reading was seventy-seven. Joseph, however, failed to take into consideration the portions of the two tapes he was forced to tie into a knot in order to get both of them around me. Consequently the pants I subsequently fed myself into burst as soon as I buttoned them, sending a small metal button-turned-projectile against the mirror before which I was standing and back against the eye of Joseph. As Joseph held his head and fell back, I retreated to the rear of the store where, with great difficulty, I got myself out of the two-legged tent and back into my holey faded corduroys, a veritable landscape. Joseph was near the door when I trudged out and, glaring at me through the fingers over the eye, said, "I think I may go blind." I replied with a whisper, "It's the button's fault, not mine," then made my way to the sidewalk as quickly as possible.

Each stair seems to be a little crooked and the whole seems to narrow as it rises. It is possible that the carpenter was a stupid man who kept breaking the end off his extension ruler for one reason or another. I imagine him at mid-stairs, for example, snapping off a piece in order to make a scraper to take dog dung off his shoe—another piece for picking food out of his teeth, another to pry open his toolbox, and so on. In measuring he failed to take into account the inches lost, just as Joseph, climbing to the shelf containing the jumbo sizes, failed to add three to seventy-seven. Both of them, then, ended up short of inches like the Jewish gentleman in the story about the Swede, the Irishman and the Jew.

They all bet a bartender that the consummate length of their penises at rest surpassed eighteen inches. The Jewish gentleman, it turned out, provided only three inches, plus a fraction. Yet they won. The Jewish gentleman silenced the mocking laughter of his friends and the bartender by pointing out that without him the three customers would now be paying for their beers. To the Jewish gentleman's great credit, it was not he but the bartender who observed, "It's not what you have but how you use it that counts."

And, for me, it is getting up those stairs and not speculating on same that matters. I will therefore push aside a volume of associations, speculations, calculations, projections, addings, subtractings, whys and wherefores, mights and maybes, whups and tittles, whats and bon mots, what nexts and so ons, and raise my massive right leg to step number one.

Oooofff!

I have clearly failed to account for the railing to my right which bends against this ecstasy of bulk. With its narrow bars it has an airy look, a spacious look, and I have been deceived. Indeed, the wall to my left, light in color, birch by the look of it, seemed farther from the railing than it really is. I am caught between both like toothpaste in the neck of a tube, as unable to get myself back down as the toothpaste to get itself back into the tube.

Perhaps not. Perhaps I could lower my foot and sort of pop back to the floor.

But there above me, like the Matterhorn, lies the landing.

I will continue.

Hold breath. Lean a little toward the wall. Raise leg.

Rrrrrccckkk.

Oh oh. A sliver of birch has entered my shirt and holds me between two and three. A warning.

And I still have choices.

Choice one: continue up.

Choice two: back down.

Choice three . . .

There is no choice three. There is, in fact, no choice two. I cannot see behind me. I would have to lower my foot blindly. I might slip. A slip and tumble for me, even through the space of approximately eight inches the lowest parts of me, feet, would travel to reach the floor, could be as disastrous as another man's fall from the roof of a one-story building. There is no choice three and there is no choice two. There is no leaping over the railing or no plunging through it, no choices four and five, and, for that matter, no six, seven, eight, nine, or ten. An infinity of impossibilities. Nothing to do but . . .

Zzzzzzttt.

There goes the side of my shirt and a little piece of underwear, but at least I am on stair three.

What was that?

A squeak.

More of a creak.

"You imagine most of what you hear," Mother said the night I told her there were sounds in the basement. She herself was quite content to believe that ghosts and angels actually walked through the halls and bedrooms of our house. Though Father has been dead for years, she had had a long conversation with him in the bathroom just the day before I heard basement noises. "Say your prayers and go to sleep," she told me. I said my prayers and went to sleep. In the morning she went down and found that every sock, jar, and memento had been taken. The burglar or burglars had also removed the washing machine, the clothesline, the faucets on the sink, the sink itself, all loose nails in the posts and beams, screws, screwdrivers, hammer, trunks, and even the panes from the windows. "God's will be done," she said after coming up the stairs, and then she made me kneel down with her and say a rosary in thanks that the two of us hadn't also been toted off.

Mrrrrmmmkkk.

Four.

There it is again. Am perhaps too susceptible to perceptible squeaks and creaks. Imagined or not imagined, it may be best to ignore. Was mother not correct in ignoring me when I heard sounds in the basement? Had she gone down to investigate, she might have taken a blow in the mouth, just as I, in attempting to go back down now, might fracture one or both buttocks. The hell with going down. I'm . . .

Phweeeeezzzz!

(five from eleven equals six)

. . . nearly halfway to the top.

On, on and on.

Did the Pope give up when they threatened to foreclose his mortgage on the Vatican?

He did not.

Did the President give up when they burned to cinders the embassy at Istanbul?

He did not.

Did Mother give up when one of the five-pound jars of peanut butter she brought home for me every week slipped through the bottom of her shopping bag and smashed three of her toes?

She did not.

What is the descent of man, or for that matter ascent, if not: *not giving up.*

There you are.

Wouffff!

Six.

Oh, the creaks and squeaks of this stairway are the creaks and squeaks of life itself. Here today and gone tomorrow. What would we be without noises and pains? It's onward and upward. I've spent my years doubting. I've doubted even Mother. There's nothing to match the love of a mother for her son. I'm going to get to the top of those stairs. A quitter never wins and a winner never quits. I may come down from the top of those stairs and try out for the Olympic Games as a sprinter, or become a glider pilot. Life has a way of taking care of itself. But I do dearly wish that noise would stop.

My legs are up and down again.

I am on stair seven.

Am I growing thicker by the step or are these stairs actually narrowing? The one I'm now on feels like a seesaw. There's a need to spread my legs upon it and open my back cheeks for an essential release of gas.

Isn't it funny how the mind works? I think, for example, how, with a nice steady blow-out, I might propel myself up another step or two —prrrrrrouppp, thump, thump. Heh. The imagination is like a toy. A worthy playmate. But has nothing to do with the job of getting to the top.

The stairway I hear creaking is a stairway of the mind.

Oh, the defeats I'd suffer if I took seriously all the plinks and plonks of the imagination.

Eight, is it?

Arrghhuuffff.

Not quite, for the seesaw movement of seven has kept me from getting right foot quite onto eight.

Will try again.

Of course.

Mmmmmmmnnnnnnnggggghhhhhh.

Cannot get foot over top of next step.

Don't give up.

Never give up.

Quaint sound. Like a wooden ferry boat trying to get itself into a wooden slip.

And another. Me.

Ahhhhhhhh.

I'm at least two pounds lighter because of it. Like Mother's distant thunder. I never heard it the way she did. She heard something when the burglars were in the basement and said it was thunder. My sound sounds like thunder but smells like smelly cheese. Well, we've all got our odors. Just like the animals. Mine is a mixture of beer krause and Monterey Jack. It hangs around too, giving the air a kind of familiarity. Anybody who knows me could find me by it.

Enough dillydallying.

There's a journey to be completed.

This time I'll put just a little weight on the railing, raise my leg and . . .

Eeeeeeeeeeeyowwwwwwwwwww!

KAAAAAAAAAAAHHHHHHHHHHRRRRRRRROOOOO-OOMMMMMMMMMMMMM!

I rest alive, though bruised, in a pile of rubble beneath a fragment of landing near the rotted skeleton of a former staircase and am unable to move anything but the smallest toe of my left foot which I will continue to move and to move and to move until the time comes when I can no longer move it.

Constants

"If I was in charge up there, I'd clean them out. Hoses. Gas. If that didn't work I'd use guns."

Bread, beer, cigarettes. I wrote a check: $5.27, amount of purchase.

He paused before shoving the beer into the bag. "You like this salami?"

"Better than the other."

"Too bitter on the tongue."

"Peter's?"

"Yeah, yeah. Peter's."

I handed him the check.

"Gar," he said, "you spelled it wrong."

"P-e-t-e-r?"

"Delicatessen. How do you spell it?"

"The way it's on the check."

"Garff." He rubbed his sleeve across his nose. The big hairs coming out hung off to the left before he rubbed. They hung off to the right afterwards. "College people. None of you know how."

"I'll change it."

"No. The guy at the bank don't care. He don't know anyway. Does it the same. He says throw 'em in the river. The ones that march. My wife's cousin. Two kids. Comes in from Canton."

Around the corner and down a block was a little grocery. Sometimes there was a girl behind the counter. She looked about fifteen.

In the middle of the block beyond the grocery was a milk bar, Alfred's. Alfred came from Mitchell's Point, Colorado. He said he once trapped muskrats. The girl from the grocery was sitting in a school desk at the back of Alfred's. Her mother was taking her place in the grocery store. I smiled at the girl. She looked at Alfred. Alfred said there was no money in it. I said in what. He said trapping muskrats. He said you probably haven't thought about it. He said whoever thinks about trapping muskrats.

Before I left the house she said, "Why did you marry me?"

I got up and took her neck in my hands.

When I let go she said she didn't have a husband. "I haven't got a husband!"

"Shit on you," I said.

She said, "They're in there listening."

I said, "Shit on you."

She said, "Stop that!"

I said, "Shit on you."

She said, "I am having another one in seven months. How do you like that?"

Then it was over. I went out and ended up at Alfred's. He had a blue mark under one eye. He said he had been bitten by a muskrat. He said there wasn't a lot of money in the milk bar but it was clean work. He said where you from. I said you mean originally and he said okay originally and I said, "San Francisco."

"I was there once. That's a great place. I was in the Navy. I went down this street with my buddies from the ship. These women in nee-yawn lights you went in and they charged like hell for drinks but these broads like coming up to you all the time I'm forty now but then it was like I never saw before making passes at us one guy went out and didn't come back we thought up to some room but he didn't come back when he was supposed to and then the next day on the ship the S.P.'s brought him he got rolled you know I was going to go out with this fat Mexican but she wanted thirty bucks or something and I'm glad I didn't. Better watch what I say with her in here."

She had on a very short dress and didn't cross her legs and was looking at me. Sometimes I went into the grocery when she was working alone at night. Now she smiled. Not at Alfred but me. I smiled at her again. She didn't stop looking this time. She might have been fourteen.

"So you're from San Francisco."

"Yes." I was having a carton of chocolate milk. He had offered to make me a shake. I didn't want a shake.

"God damn, that's some town."

The sky in this town is often black. Maybe high clouds or maybe you just can't see the stars as well as in other places. Bumbo wanted me to take him for a walk one night. He said let's count the stars. He called them tars. We went out but there were no stars.

Peter said call me Pete. "You know those others up there call me Mr. Dracopolous and I just about drop my load. I been here all my life and everyone calls me Pete. What you call each other up there, first name or last?"

"First, usually."

"What do you teach?"

"Teach?"

"You must teach something."

For a moment I couldn't remember what I taught. The general area is humanities. There are many courses. I said the first thing that came to mind. "History."

"Be darned."

In the afternoon high school kids drink soda pops at the back of the grocery when the girl is behind the counter. At night she is alone. I buy the *New York Times* there on Sundays. I stop at the delicatessen or Alfred's at night. When we fight Marcy doesn't shop. Sometimes we need things the grocery has. When I go into the store the girl doesn't look at me. She doesn't talk. When I say what I want she gets it. Once she was humming when I walked in.

Now she got up and left Alfred's. First she put her paper cup down on the counter beside my carton near where I was standing.

"That's a good looking kid," Alfred said when she went out. I thought he'd say more but he didn't.

"You come bring your wife down here some night," Peter said. "I make you a couple of pastramis like you never had."

Alfred said, "How come you left?"

"Graduate school. Got married. Then the job here."

"Yeah," Peter said, "I get my bread in Massena. They got no good bread in this town."

Alfred said, "Took a walk down by this fort before they separated me. Don't know what the hell the name of it was."

"Presidio? The old Presidio?"

"That's it. That's it."

Peter said, "My god damn wife makes Greek bread but won't make it for the store. You can't get a good rye. She's a lazy horse. You ever see her in here?"

"No."

"That's what I mean. Won't ever see her. Ever. Know what I mean? Goes to a movie Tuesday night. Up to her mother's place Thursday. On the phone the rest of the time. House smells half the time. Little place in back there. Ever see it?"

"No."

Alfred said, "The view you could see all the way across I mean even more than Alcatraz to these hills I think there was an island in the bay isn't there an island. . . ."

"Angel's Island."

"Yeah and then after that little towns over there I don't know the names but what I'm saying is prettier than hell with all that blue water but the Atlantic is green which beats the hell out of me the sky the same on both sides but the water is a different color better though than no water which we mostly have in Colorado. Or here. If I was married I'd settle in San Francisco. No question."

Peter said, "Put it out on a hill between here and Canton you would think it'd be worth seven, eight thousand and put a big enough yard around, maybe a few cows and I bet it would be more, but stuck to a store and in an alley like it is it's not worth two god damn cents."

Alfred said, "They gave you rides on these buses for eight-fifty take you all over. . . ."

"Tour buses."

"Tour buses, yeah."

We were in bed when it started. "Why don't you say things when we're doing it? Who is it you think about? Tell me who it is. I know you think about someone. Maybe it's a boy, one of those you teach or one of those others that march all the time. Why do you say you're on their side? It's probably got to do with sex. Why don't you grow up?"

Peter said, "Why don't they throw out those ones that march around."

"I don't know."

"I'd do it. I wouldn't let nobody put no pressure on me. The other ones who come in for sandwiches are okay. I don't let all that hair in here. What they got they want more of. Who pays their tuition? This was a quiet town once."

"It still is."

"Yeah. But not like this. It's not the other ones I mind. If they didn't come in here after classes for sandwiches and stuff I wouldn't have a business. That kind I can put up with."

I went to the grocery store. I asked her for one of those chewy candy bars there.

She got one.

I paid her. I opened the wrapper and bit off one piece. I put it in my mouth and chewed, looking at her.

She watched me. Then she looked down at the rest of the candy bar in my hand.

I raised it to her.

She leaned forward and took a bite.

We chewed, looking at each other, fast at first and then slow.

When she finished she wiped her tongue over her lips. She began to giggle.

I said, "Do you know what I'd like to do with you?"

She said, "I think so." She giggled.

"Where is your mother?"

"At the back of the store reading."

"I'll be back some time."

She giggled again.

"Think about me coming back."

She giggled again.

Marcy was asleep but I woke her crossing the floor, which is squeaky.

I said, "You want a piece of candy?"

She said, "My stomach hurts."

When I got close to the bed I saw she was spread-eagled on it, taking up a lot of room.

I went into the children's room and slept beside Bumbo.

The Thumb

I cannot move. The condition has embraced me for seeming years. In fact, it has been much less, to know which is to know little. It's the seeming and not the fact that permeates.

I am in a time and place. My thumb is stuck behind half of a small butterfly affair called lock. I am in a room, at the door. In appearance a man about to leave the room. Who can't.

Were I outdoors and the butterfly a real butterfly, but magic, and had somehow gotten hold of my thumb, it would be the same, the very same, a condition in which I would have found myself. There may be extensions, other butterflies. There may be extensions everywhere. More than butterflies.

On that wall are those books. I should speak about those books. When I have entered this room their covers accost me like an army: myriad of colors, at attention, in full dress—squads, platoons, battalions. As if they might come down and liberate. As if.

Impossible. They have been as if a ton upon my head, squiring me downward ever downward like a corkscrew into this hard floor. I have read from most of them and they have drawn me down to where the sawdust lies gray, forgotten nails sleep against beams, and spiders go mad in the absence of flies. They have driven me a few inches out of my time and place. I always return.

The books. They regard me now as if. As if smiling.

I would say so.

Curse the books, the condition, the lock, the room, I give it all away: they are mere excuses. A more honest man would have begun: *I have this and thus to say. Listen.*

I came close.

We live, unfortunately, in a phase of old habits; one must still present oneself in garments.

Quite.

Forgive me, but we have become accustomed to illusion, to the weaving of illusions. The web of the spider beneath the floor is nothing more than its own survival kit, yet we project art. The plans of character X in novel Y by which was foiled antagonist Z are held against the web and an analogy occurs: *like a web, it was artful, sinister*. The spider, however, had nothing, *had nothing*, in mind. We pretend. Not interested in essences at all.

It is where we don't get—i.e., the causes of the antagonism toward books and its value or lack of it, the being here, the going where—that has fundament. At least vague fundament. An essence beyond dictionaries. I shall not get into it. I could never hope to. And if I could it would be only illusion anyway. Books are many things. Books are metaphors for themselves. Only in that sense are they sure to rise above zero in the lasting record of the human species.

What matter the thumb?

Ai, yes. The thumb is swelling now around the brass lock, which has again refused to go its complete clockwise circle, will not release the thumb and me. If that is fact and more than fact, then all those books can do nothing to change it.

Here. I fiddled with my wife last night but pictured the neighbor girl, with whom I flew to an orgasmic circus. I shall now proclaim that that is why I got my thumb stuck in this lock. On acquitting myself of the fantasy with its satisfaction, once-removed, I devised an unseeable cage. It has now found correlation in the lock on the door of my office. I insist that I am here to serve sentence against my sin in bed with wife. That is how I take it to be.

Don't believe me.

The facts are these: again and again I have returned to this room and again and again this room has in one way or another contained me against myself. There are reasons and reasons, never the same.

No matter. Eventually I always find my way out, release from desk, chair, books, all except.

There was a dream. In it a dark Frenchman with a thin moustache entered a maiden's bedroom in Waterford. I, in the dream, was the maiden.

Go.

But he stayed. Fell upon me, hands turning to crab claws.

Stay.

But he fled.

I wept.

What was solved?

I leave this, a scrap, a chocolate drop at the center of a cookie, a piece of gravel caught between the first two toes, the "o" in the middle of a long word, a drop of saliva on the lip of one of the women who did not drive me to this room: one lives, pretends he knows, reads the fictions and philosophies of some who don't: tolerates, works, empties, sleeps, walks, smells, and hangs on, examining the whole with an energy that is marvelous.

Ici! The thumb! The thumb has freed itself. The thumb has freed itself intact. Of course, of course, of course. *Ici! Voila!* The thumb is now free. It is necessary and should have been expected.

I, however, remain.

A paperback original

A SEASON FOR UNNATURAL CAUSES

Stories by Philip F. O'Connor

Nine stories and a novella, "The Escape Artist," called by Guy Owen a *tour de force* and by Stanley Elkin "genuinely good, O'Connor's best writing yet." O'Connor's first volume was widely praised. Commenting on it in *Saturday Review,* H. L. Van Brunt wrote, "If you can't find an absorbing story in *Old Morals, Small Continents, Darker Times,* you probably don't like to read." He added, "If a major commercial publisher doesn't pick up the option to O'Connor's next book, someone is missing a hell of a good bet." In a review for the *Philadelphia Bulletin,* novelist Christopher Davis characterized *Old Morals* as "capturing the life of people, the presence of places, and the beauty of talk — so much so that we do not realize at once that we are in the very scene of our origins."

PHILIP F. O'CONNOR is professor of English at Bowling Green State University, where he helped develop the graduate and undergraduate programs in creative writing. He is a native of San Francisco, and holds master's degrees from San Francisco State College and the University of Iowa. His stories have been published in many journals, including *Kansas Quarterly, Southern Review, Quartet, Transatlantic Review, Western Humanities Review,* and *Wisconsin Review.* One of his stories was included in Martha Foley's *Best American Short Stories, 1971,* and his first collection won the 1971 Iowa School of Letters Award for Short Fiction. In making the final selection in that competition, to which more than 250 manuscripts were submitted, novelist and critic George P. Elliott wrote, "O'Connor has the true Irish gift of telling a tale for all it's worth, but he also has the sophistication of narrative technique. . . . His stories are taut and painful too; that is to say, they ring true."

A Season for Unnatural Causes is one of the first four volumes in the Illinois Short Fiction series. The others are: *Crossings* by Stephen Minot; *Curving Road* by John Stewart; and *Such Waltzing Was Not Easy* by Gordon Weaver.

This book is also available in a casebound edition @ $6.95.

AN ILLINI BOOK FROM THE UNIVERSITY OF ILLINOIS PRESS

Photo by J. R. Gordon

ISBN 0-252-00531-7